GOOD MANNERS

A man can lose patience. I reached across that bar and grabbed myself a handful of shirt and jerked that bartender half over his bar.

The grip I'd taken was well up at his throat, and I held him there and shook him real good a time or two, and when his face started to turn blue, I slammed him back so's he hit that back bar like he'd been throwed by a bronco. He slammed into it, and a couple of bottles toppled off and busted.

"Fix the girl some soup," I said, matter-of-factly, "and be careful what tone you use around a lady."

LOGAN SACKETT IS IN TOWN!

Bantam Books by Louis L'Amour
Ask your bookseller for the books you have missed.

Louis L'Amour
Ride the Dark Trail

BANTAM BOOKS
TORONTO • NEW YORK • LONDON • SYDNEY • AUCKLAND

To
Uncle Dan Freeman,
of St. Cloud

RIDE THE DARK TRAIL
A Bantam Book / June 1972

2nd printing . . . . . July 1972	14th printing . . . . . May 1979
3rd printing . . . October 1972	15th printing . . . . . June 1980
4th printing . . . . . July 1973	16th printing . . February 1981
5th printing . . . January 1974	17th printing . . . . . July 1981
6th printing . . February 1974	18th printing . . . . . June 1982
7th printing . September 1975	19th printing . . . . March 1983
8th printing . . . . . May 1976	20th printing . . . August 1983
9th printing . . . . . May 1976	21st printing . . . . . June 1984
10th printing . December 1977	22nd printing . . . August 1984
11th printing . . . . . July 1978	23rd printing . . . . . June 1986
12th printing . . . January 1979	24th printing . . . . . April 1987
13th printing . . . January 1979	25th printing . December 1987

ISBN 0-553-25512-6

Published simultaneously in the United States and Canada

Bantam Books are published by Bantam Books, a division of
Bantam Doubleday Dell Publishing Group, Inc. Its trademark,
consisting of the words "Bantam Books" and the portrayal of
a rooster, is Registered in U.S. Patent and Trademark Office
and in other countries. Marca Registrada. Bantam Books,
666 Fifth Avenue, New York, New York 10103.

PRINTED IN THE UNITED STATES OF AMERICA

KR   34 33 32 31 30 29 28 27 26 25

1

The old house stood on the crest of a knoll and it was three hundred yards to the main gate. No shrubbery or trees obscured the view, nor was there any cover for a half mile beyond.

The house was old, weather-beaten, wind-harried, and long unpainted. By night no light shone from any window, and by day no movement could be seen, but the watchers from the hill a half mile away were not fooled.

"She's there, all right. You lay a hand on that gate and you'll damned soon know she's there. She's setting up there in that old house and she can shoot."

Behind the house, the mountains lifted abruptly, steep, ragged slopes broken by ledges and dikes, covered with rough growth and dead-fall timber. Directly behind the house, only the top spread of its walls visible, lay the mouth of a canyon opening into the mountains beyond.

"Old Man Talon built that house to last, and when he built it, it was the finest house between New Orleans and Frisco. He had thirty tough hands then . . . a reg'lar army."

"How many's she got now?" Matthew asked.

"Not more'n two or three. The best of her land and the sources of all her water lie back of the house, and there's no way to get at it except right through the ranch yard. And that ol' devil ain't about to let anybody get by."

"She's got to sleep, ain't she?" Brewer asked.

"She sleeps, I suppose, but nobody ain't figured out when. Lay a finger on that gate and she'll part your brisket with a fifty-caliber bullet.

1

"The way folks tell it Old Man Talon figured someday they'd have to stand siege so he laid by enough ammunition and grub, too, to supply an army."

The three men eyed the house, irritation mixed with admiration, then turned to the coffeepot on their small fire.

"Flanner's right. The on'y way is to keep at her, every hour of every day and night. Sooner or later she's got to sleep, and then we'll get in. Behind that house in those canyons there's some of the finest land anywhere, watered by mountain streams and walled by mountains. No ol' woman's got the right to keep that land to herself, to say nothin' of the hundred thousand acres out here on the plains that they lay claim to."

"How come they got so much?"

"Talon was the first white man to settle in this country. When he and his partner came out here there was nothing but Indians and wild game. His partner was after fur, but not Talon. He seen this place and latched onto it, knowing that a hundred thousand acres out here was no good without water from the mountains.

"Talon and his partner built a cabin and wintered here, the partner taking all the fur, Talon keeping house and land. Come spring, the partner pulled his stakes, but Talon stayed on, fit Injuns, hunted buffalo, trapped a mite, and caught himself some wild horses.

"A few years passed by and the wagon trains started coming through. Talon had grub. He had raised him some corn, and he had jerked venison by the ton, and he swapped with the travelers for their wore-out cattle.

"He held his stock back in the canyons where he had no need for hands, and on that rich grass with plenty of water he built himself some herds. Somewhere along the line he taken off for the east and married up with this Tennessee hill woman. The way I hear it she was some kin to his old partner."

"Talon's dead?"

"Dry-gulched, they say. Nobody knows who done it."

"Is it true? Did she bust Flanner's knees?"

"Uh-huh. Flanner figured when her old man died that Em Talon would pull for the States, but she never done it. Moreover, she had her an idea Flanner had killed Talon.

"Flanner came out to run her off, and she let him come right on in. When he was maybe a hundred yards off she stopped him with a bullet to his feet and then she told him for what he was . . . or what she figured him to be.

"She said she wasn't going to kill him, she wanted him to live a hundred years, regrettin' ever' day of his life what he'd done. Then she cut down on him with that big fifty and busted both knees. Jake Flanner ain't walked a step since, not without them crutches."

The wind picked up, slapping their slickers against their chaps, and the three men began rigging their tarp to hold against the wind. It was going to be a bad night.

From time to time they turned to look at the great, gloomy old house, far away on its wind-swept knoll, bleak, lonely and harsh, like the woman who waited within.

Emily Talon leaned the Sharps against the doorjamb and peered through the shutters. Cold rain slanted from a darkening sky. Served them right, she reflected grimly, they'd have them a miserable night out there. She walked back to kindle a fire and put on water for tea.

From time to time she returned to peer through the shutters. It wouldn't be so bad if she had somebody to spell her, but the last of them died, and she'd buried him with her own hands, and now she was alone.

She was old now, old and tired. If only the boys would come home! She wanted both of them to come, but she told herself she was an evil old woman to want Milo most of all, Milo because he was a fast hand with a gun and mean. She needed a mean man now, to handle that bunch, and Milo could do it.

3

Milo taken after her kin. No Talon was ever that mean. The Talons were strong men, hard-working men and smarter than most. They were fighters, too, game as they came—those she'd met or heard tell of—but Milo was mean.

Any man who crossed Milo Talon was taking a risk. He was her youngest and a good boy, but he'd take water for no man. If you wished for trouble with Milo you'd best come a-shootin'.

Em Talon was tall and gaunt. Her one regret as a girl was that she fell just short of six feet. Her brothers had all been six-footers, and she'd wished to be at least that tall, but she'd fallen short by a quarter of an inch.

Her dress was old, gray, and nondescript. Her shoes had belonged to pa, but big as they were they were comfortable on her feet. Em Talon was sixty-seven years old and she had lived on the MT ranch for forty-seven of those years.

She'd been living alone in a cabin in the Cumberlands when pa came riding up to the door. A fine, handsome man he was, in store-bought clothes, shining boots, and riding a blood-bay gelding that stepped like a dancer.

He drew up outside the fence near where she was cutting flowers. "My name is Talon," he said, "and I'm looking for Em Sackett."

"What do you want with her?"

"I've come courting, and I've come a long way. I was partner to a cousin of hers out in the shining mountains."

She studied him with thoughtful eyes. "I am Emily Sackett," she said, "and you won't do much courtin' a-settin' up on that horse. Get down and come in."

She was twenty years old that summer, by mountain standards an old maid, but two weeks later they were married and had a fine honeymoon down New Orleans way.

Then she rode west beside Talon into a land of buffalo and Indians. When she rode up to the ranch house she

4

could not believe what she saw. The house was there, larger than any other she had ever seen, even in New Orleans . . . and there wasn't even a cabin or dugout within a hundred miles, nor a town within two hundred or more.

She was called Em and Talon's name began with a T, so they took MT for a brand, now known far and wide as the Empty.

Pa was gone now, but it was many a fine year they'd had together. Pa was dead, and the man who'd killed him sat yonder in the town with two broken knees and a heart eaten with hatred for the woman who crippled him.

Flanner had hated Talon from the moment he saw him. Hated and envied him, for Talon already had what Flanner wanted. Jake Flanner decided the easiest way to come by what he wanted was to take what Talon had.

At first he tried to frighten the grim-jawed old man, but there was no fright in him that anybody ever located, so he had killed him or had him killed, sure that Em would pull out when her husband was dead. No woman could ever stand in his way . . . but there she stood.

It was cold in the big old house, and the rooms were dark and shadowed. A little of the last light of evening filtered through the heavy shutters. The house was dusty, and the air was stale and old. When a woman had to stand guard all day little time was left for housekeeping. She who had kept the neatest house in the Cumberland hills now had only a kitchen in which she dared live.

Talon had been a builder, as his family had been. He had come down from French Canada to build a steamboat for river traffic. The first of his line to live west of the Atlantic had been a ship-wright, and since then they had all been ship-wrights, mill-wrights, bridge-builders and workers with timber.

Pa had built keel boats, several steamboats, a dozen mills and bridges, and finally this house. He built with his own hands and he built to last. He had felled the timber, seasoned it, and shaped each piece with cunning hands. He dug the cellar himself and walled it with native stone, and he had prepared for every eventuality he could think of.

Looking out now Em saw the men huddled under their tarp, lashed by wind and rain. In each flash of lightning she could see something else. Every rock—a dozen at least—was painted white with black numerals on the side facing the house. The numerals represented the range, the number of yards from the door to that particular rock. Pa was a thoughtful man, and he preferred his shooting to be accurate.

Yet now pa was gone and she was alone, and her sons did not know how desperately she needed them.

She was exhausted. Her bones ached, and when she sat down she only managed to get up with an effort. Even making tea was a struggle, and sometimes when she eased her tired body into a chair she thought how easy it would be just to stay, to never make the effort to rise again.

It would be easy, too easy, and nothing had ever been easy for her.

She had nursed three children with a rifle across her knees. She had driven two cowhands back to the ranch, both of them gut-shot and moaning.

The first man she killed had been a renegade Kiowa, the last man a follower of Jake Flanner. There had been several in between, but she never counted.

They were going to win. She could not last forever, and Jake Flanner could hire more men. He could keep them out there until exhaustion destroyed her and her will to resist.

So far she had managed catnaps, which had been enough since the old often require less sleep than the young. Yet one day she would nap a little too long and they would come up the trail and put an end to her.

They would fire the house. That was the simplest way for them. They could then say the house caught fire and that she died with it. The explanation would be plausible enough, and whoever came to investigate—if anyone came—would be anxious to get the job over with and go home.

The nearest law was miles away, and the trails were rough.

Emily Talon had but one hope. That the boys would come home. It was for that she lived, it was for that she fought.

"Hold the ranch for the boys," pa had always said. Had he any idea how long it would be?

Of their six sons, only two were living when pa died. The oldest died at sixteen when a horse fell on him, and the second had been killed by Indians on the plains of western Nebraska. A third had died only four weeks after birth, and the fourth had died in a gun battle with rustlers right here on the Empty.

The two who remained were far apart in years as well as their thinking. Barnabas had wanted to go away to Canada to school, and had done so. When his school was nearly completed he had gone off to France to finish and had lived there with relatives. He had served in the French army, or something of the kind.

Milo was younger by eight years. Where Barnabas was cool, thoughtful and studious, Milo was impetuous, energetic, and quick-tempered. At fifteen he had hunted down and killed the rustler who killed his brother on the Empty. A year later he killed a would-be herd-cutter in the Texas Panhandle. At seventeen he had gone off to join the Confederate army, had become a sergeant, then a lieutenant. The war ended and they heard no more of him.

Nor had they heard from Barnabas. His last letter had come from France several years before.

Em Talon added sticks to the fire, then shuffled into the front hall to peer through the shutters. There were

7

intermittent flashes of heat lightning, and she saw no movement, heard no sound other than the rain.

She feared rain, for during a heavy rain storm she could not hear or see nearly so well. And her watchers were snug in their holes under the rocks.

Flanner and his men were not yet aware of the part played by her watchers. Inside the gate, yet near it, there were piles of rocks gathered from the prairie and adopted as homes by several families of marmots. Quick to whistle when anything strange moved near, they had warned her on more than one occasion, and her ears were tuned to their sound.

Returning to her chair she eased herself down and leaned back with a sigh. There had been a time when she had ridden free as the wind across these same plains, ridden beside Talon, feeling the wind in her hair and the sun warm upon her back.

During those first hard years she had worked with rope and horse like any cowhand. She hunted meat for the table, helped to stretch the first wire brought on the place, and helped pa at the windlass when he dug his well.

She was old now, and tired. The long, wakeful nights left her trembling, yet she was not afraid. When they came after her in the end she hoped but for one thing, that she would awaken in time to get off a shot.

Nothing had frightened her in the old days, but then pa had always been close by, and now pa was gone.

Slowly her tired muscles relaxed. Thunder rumbled out there, and the heat lightning showed brief flashes through the cracks of the shutters. She must take another look soon. In a little while.

Her eyes closed . . . only for a minute, she told herself, only for one brief, wonderful minute.

2

Nobody needed to tell me what I needed was a place out of the rain and a good, hot meal. Maybe a drink. The long-geared, raw-boned roan I was riding had run himself into the ground and was starting to flounder. We'd come a fur piece together, and we'd come fast. It began to look like I'd out-run trouble for the time, but then I wasn't going to make any bets until I'd seen the cards.

Lightning flashed and there looked to be rain-wet roofs off there. A cold drop of rain slipped down the back of my neck and down my spine, and I swore.

I'd no idea whose slicker I was wearing, but I was surely pleased to have it instead of leaving it with him. Anyway, he would be nursing a headache for the next few days and should ought to stay in bed.

It was a town off there, sure enough. Or what passed for a town in this country.

There were six or eight buildings that might be stores or saloons and a scattering of shacks folks might live in. Lights shone from a set of four windows. There was a "Hotel" sign over two of them, so I turned in at the livery stable.

Seemed to be nobody around so I found myself an empty stall, stripped the gear from the roan, rubbed him dry with a few handfuls of hay, and then taking rifle and saddlebags I walked up front.

Of a sudden there was a pounding of hoofs and a team came tearing around the corner and into the street, coming at a belly-to-the-ground dead run. Me, I'd started for the saloon in that hotel building and I jumped clear just in time to keep from being run over.

The driver pulled up in front of the hotel and got down, a wisp of a girl in a rain-wet dress that clung to a mighty cute shape. She tied the team and went inside.

When I fetched open the door and came in quiet she was the center of attention, all wet and bedraggled in the middle of the floor.

There weren't more than five or six men in the place. A big, blond man wearing a red shirt and a nasty kind of smile stood at the bar.

"It's that waif-girl who taken up workin' for Spud Tavis," he was saying. "Looks like she run off an' lef' ol' Spud, an' him expectin' so much of her, too."

"I would like to talk to the owner of this place," the girl said. "Please, will somebody tell me where he is? I want a job."

"Not fat enough for my taste." The speaker was a short, thick-set man with black hair. "I like 'em plump so's you can get hold of something. This one's too skinny."

Me, I closed the door soft and just stood there, liking nothing I saw, but wishing for no trouble. Three of the men in that saloon were trying to pay no mind to what was happening, but a body could see they didn't hold with it. Neither did I.

Nobody ever held Logan Sackett up to be no hero. Me, I've run the wild trails since who flung the chunk, and I've picked up a few horses here and yon, and some cattle, too. I've ridden the back trails with the wild bunch and from time to time I've had folks comin' down my trail with a noose hung out for hangin', but I never bothered no womenfolk.

"You, there," the big blond man said to her, "you come here to me."

"I'll do no such thing." She was scared but she had spunk. "I'm a good girl, Len Spivey, and you know it!"

10

He chuckled, then straightened slowly from the bar. "You comin', or do I come after you?"

"Leave her alone," I said.

For a moment, nothing moved. It was like I'd busted a window or something the way everybody stopped and turned to look at me.

Well, they hadn't much to see. I'm a big man, weighing around two-fifteen most of the time and most of it in my chest and shoulders. I was wearing a handlebar mustache and a three-day growth of beard. My hair hadn't been trimmed in a coon's age and that beat up old hat was showing a bullet hole picked up back of yonder. My slicker was hanging open, my leather chaps was wet, and my boots rundown at heel so's those big-roweled California spurs were draggin' a mite.

"What did you say?" That blond man was staring at me like he couldn't believe it. Seemed like nobody ever stopped him doing what he had a mind to.

"I said leave her alone. Can't you see the lady is wet, tired, an' lookin' for a room for herself?"

"You stay the hell out of this, mister. If she wants a room she can have mine, and me with it."

I turned to her. "Ma'am, you pay no mind to such talk. You just set down yonder and I'll see you have something warm to eat an' drink."

That blond man wasn't fixed to like me very much. "Stranger," he said, "you'd better back off an' take another look. This here ain't your town. If I was you I'd straddle whatever I rode in here and git off down the road before I lose patience."

Now we Clinch Mountain Sacketts ain't noted for gentle ways. The way I figure it is if a man is big enough to open his mouth he's big enough to take the consequences, and I was getting tired of talk.

Stepping over to an empty table I drawed back a chair. "Ma'am, you just set here." I walked over to the bar, and, turning to the man behind it, I said, "Fix the lady a bowl of hot soup and some coffee."

"Mister," he rested both hands on the bar, his expression as unpleasant as that other gent's, "I wouldn't fix that—"

A man can lose patience. I reached across that bar and grabbed myself a handful of shirt and jerked that bartender half over his bar.

The grip I'd taken was well up at his throat and I held him there and shook him real good a time or two and when his face started to turn blue, I slammed him back so's he hit that back bar like he'd been throwed by a bronco. He slammed into it and a couple of bottles toppled off and busted. "Fix that soup," I said matter-of-factly, "and be careful what tone you use around a lady."

That Len Spivey, he just stood there, kind of surprised, I take it. I'd been keeping him in mind, and the others, too. Nothing in my life had left me trusting of folks.

"I don't think you understand," the blond man said, "I'm Len Spivey!"

Seems like every cow town has some two-by-twice would-be bad man.

"You forget about it, son," I said, "and I'll promise not to tell nobody!"

Well, he didn't know what to do. He dearly wanted to stretch my hide but suddenly he wasn't so awful sure. It's easy to strut around playing the bad man with local folks when you know just what you can do and what they can do. But when a stranger comes into town it begins to shade off into another pattern.

"Len Spivey," the black-haired man said, "is the fastest man in this country."

"It's a small country," I said.

The bartender came with the soup and placed it on the table very carefully, then stepped back.

"Eat that," I told the girl, who looked to be no more than sixteen, and maybe less. "I'll drink the coffee."

12

Talk began and ever'body ignored us, only they didn't really. I'd been in strange towns before and knew the drill. Sooner or later one of them would make up his mind to see how tough I really was. I'd looked them over and didn't care which. They all sized up like a bunch of no-account mavericks.

"Are there any decent womenfolk around here?" I asked her. "I mean folks who aren't scared of this crowd?"

"There's only Em Talon. She ain't feered of nobody or nothing."

"Eat up," I said, "and I'll take you to her."

"Mister, you don't know what you're sayin'. That ol' woman would shoot you dead before you got the gate open. She's nailed a few, she has!"

She spooned some soup, then looked up. "Why, she shot up Jake Flanner, who owns this place! Busted both his knees!"

"Somebody mention my name?"

He stood in the door behind the corner of the bar, leaning on two crutches. He was a huge man, big but not very fat. His arms were heavy with muscle and he had big hands.

He swung around the bar, favoring one crutch a mite more than the other. A good-looking man of forty or so, he was wearing a holstered gun, and he had another, I was sure, in a shoulder holster under his coat.

"I'm Jake Flanner. I think we should have a talk."

Nobody was supposed to know he had that shoulder holster. There were mighty few of them around, and this one was set well back under his arm, and as the gun was small it could go unnoticed on a big-chested man like Jake Flanner.

A crippled man is smart to leave off wearing a gun. There's few men who would jump a cripple, and in most western towns there'd be no surer way of getting yourself nominated for a necktie party. So if this man was all loaded down with iron there had to be a reason.

13

Something about those crutches worried me, too, and how he favored one side. To use a gun he'd have to let go of a crutch.

"May I seat myself?"

"Go ahead . . . only stay out of line in case somebody decides to open the ball. I wouldn't want to kill any innocent bysitters."

"You're new around here," he said, easing himself in his chair. "Riding through?"

"More'n likely."

"Unusual for a man passing through to take up for a lady. Very gallant . . . very gallant, indeed."

"I know nothing about gallant," I said, "but a lady should be allowed to choose her comp'ny, an' should be treated like a lady until she shows she prefers different."

"Of course. I'm sure the boys meant nothing disrespectful." He taken a long look at me. "You seem to have traveled far," he said, "and judging by the looks of your horse, you've traveled fast."

"When I get shut of a place, I'm shut of it."

"Of course." He paused, stoking a pipe. "I might use a good man right here. A man," he added, "who can use a gun." He paused again. "I would surmise you are a man who has seen trouble."

"I've come a ways. And I've been up the creek an' over the ridge, if that's what you mean. I've busted broncs, roped steers, an' fit the heel flies. I've skinned buffalo and laid track an' lived with Indians, so I don't figure to be no pilgrim."

"You're just the man I've needed."

"Maybe, maybe not. You trot out your argument an' run her around the corral an' we'll see how the brand reads."

There was nothing much about this Flanner that I took to, but when a man is on the dodge with a lot of country he can't go back to right away he's in no position to be picky about folks he works for.

14

"I heard the young lady here mention Emily Talon. She runs the Empty outfit over against the mountain, and she owes me money. Now she's a mean old woman and she's got some mean cowhands and I'd like to hire you to go out there and collect for me."

"What's the matter with Spivey there? He looks like a man who's bit into a sour pickle with a sore tooth. He'd be just the man to tackle an old woman."

Spivey slammed his bottle on the bar. "Look, you!" He was so mad he spluttered.

"Spivey," I said, "you got to wait your turn. I'm in a coffee-drinkin' mood now, an' right contented to be in out of the rain. I'll take care of you when I get around to it an' not a moment sooner."

"There's fifty dollars in it," Flanner added, "and you don't have to shoot unless shot at. I'll even give you a badge to wear, so's it's official."

"Right now I need some sleep," I said, "and I ain't about to crawl back in a saddle until daybreak. How far's it out there?"

"About seven miles. It's a big, old house. The biggest an' the oldest around here." Flanner's eyes were bland. "It is an easy fifty, if you want it." He paused. "By the way . . . what shall I call you?"

"Logan . . . Logan will do."

"All right, Logan, I'll see you in the morning. Boys," he struggled to his feet, getting the crutches under his shoulders, "lay off Mister Logan. I want him around to talk to in the morning."

He swung away, moving easily on those crutches. He was a big man but he handled himself easily. Crippled or not, if'n I ever saw a dangerous man, this one was. Dangerous but smooth, mighty, mighty smooth!

"Don't you do it," the girl whispered. "Don't you help them bully that old woman."

"Thought you was scared of her. Scared to go out there?"

15

"She shoots. She's got herself a Sharps Fifty an' she will hit anything she shoots at. They're trying to take her ranch away. It's him an' them nesters. They were Johnny-come-latelies, all trying to move in on that old lady just because she's old, alone, and got the best land anywhere around."

"Are you from here?"

"Not really. My pa was one of the nesters. Pa was an honest man but he never done well. Everything he put a hand to seemed to turn sour. He wasn't much of a manager when it came to money, and he never worked no harder than the law allowed.

"There was just the two of us. Pa picked himself a piece of prairie land and tried to prove up, but the land he plowed mostly blew away and no rain came and pa took to hitting the bottle. One night coming home he fell off his horse and come morning he had pneumonia.

"I taken a job keepin' house for Spud Tavis and his youngsters, only it turned out what Spud was hunting was a woman for himself and not a housekeeper. He got almighty mean, so I got into a buckboard and came into town."

"How old are you?"

"Sixteen. Mister Logan," her voice lowered so only he could hear, "it may sound a hard thing, but if pa had to go I'm glad it was right then. Pa was going to sell something he knew to Flanner."

"About the Empty outfit?"

"Pa knew a way in. When we first came into this country we boarded a cowhand who'd worked for her. He got scared an' quit, buffaloed by Flanner's men, but before he left the country he told pa one night about a way he knew to come into the Empty outfit from behind.

"It was an Injun trail, and he come on it one time huntin' strays. It had been used a time or two, year ago. He found some sign of that, and he reckoned it was that gun-slinging kid of Talon's . . . Milo."

16

"Milo Talon? He's kin to the old woman out yonder?"

"Son. There's another boy, too, only he went off to foreign parts. Seems they had kinfolk in Canada and France. This cowhand was quite a talker, and him an' pa had knowed each other back in West Virginny."

"Your pa knew about a trail into the back of the Empty? Did he ever tell Flanner?"

"I don't think so. He figured we had to pull out and we needed a road-stake. He figured he might get a hundred dollars for it, an' we could go on to Californy or Oregon, but pa never did have no luck. That horse dropped him an' he taken sick to his death."

"That cowhand, where did he go?"

She shrugged. "He taken out. That's six, eight months ago."

"What's your name, girl?"

"I'm Pennywell Farman."

"Pennywell, I've got no money to speak of. I can't send you nowhere, but we might get you to that Em Talon. She might like to have somebody to he'p out now and again."

"We'd never get in. She'll shoot you, mister. These folks been after her place, and she'll let nobody close."

My eyes taken a look around that room and nobody seemed to be paying us no mind. All the same, I knew they were trying to listen and that they hadn't forgotten us. Pennywell went to spooning soup, and I gave thought to the fix she was in.

Me, I was a drifting man, and there was nothing around here I wanted. Right now I was figuring on wintering in Brown's Hole. I had to get shut of this girl and leave her some place she'd be safe.

I'd no idea of taking Flanner's offer. That was just a mite of stalling to get trouble off my back until I could get my horse rested and a meal in me. Seemed our only chance was that old lady yonder.

"Pennywell, when that cowhand was a-talkin' to your pa, what were you doin'?"

"Sleeping."

"Now, Penny, if I'm to help you, you got to help me. I don't figure to get myself killed, and it might be you could help that old lady. Don't you recall what that cowhand said about that trail through the back?"

She gave me a long, thoughtful look. "I think you're a good man, Mister Logan, or I'd say nothing. I think maybe I could find that trail if you'd help."

Suddenly the outer door burst open and a big man stood framed in the doorway. Len Spivey turned to look, then began to grin.

"Lookin' for your girl, Spud? There she is . . . with that stranger."

When that door opened I recognized trouble. That big man was surely on the prod and he came into the room like he figured to smash everything in sight. He was big, he was wet, and he was hoppin' mad.

"You, there! What d'you mean runnin' off with my rig? I got a notion to see you jailed for stealin' horses. You git up out o' there an' git back to the buckboard. Soon's I have a drink we'll be drivin' back home. What you need is a taste of the strap!"

"I quit!" Pennywell said firmly. "I went to care for your children, Spud Tavis, and to cook for them and you, but that was all, and you *knowed* it. You got no right to come after me thisaway!"

"By the Lord Harry, I'll show you what!"

"You heard the lady," I said mildly. "She's quit you. You're no kin to her an' you've got no rights in the matter, so leave her alone."

He reached for the girl and when he did I just kind of slapped his arm away. It caught him unexpected and spun him so's he had to take a step to keep balance.

He caught himself, his features flushed with anger,

18

and turned on me. He had a big, thick, hairy fist and he drew it back to throw a punch, but as he stepped forward there was an instant when his foot was off the ground and I let go with a sweeping, sidewise move of my foot that swept his foot over and up. He staggered and fell, hitting the floor with a bump.

He got up fast, I'll give him that. For a man of his heft he was quick, and he came right at me.

Me, I never so much as moved from my chair, only hooked my toe around the leg of the chair at the end of the table. He taken a lunge at me and I kicked the chair into his path and he came down across it, all sprawled out.

"Something the matter?" I asked. "Seems like you're kind of unsteady."

He got up more slowly, but he let his hand close over one of the broken chair legs. "Better get back against the wall," I told Pennywell, "from here on this is going to get rough."

This time he was cautious. He came toward me slowly, gripping the club in his right hand; he raised it a mite more than shoulder high and poised to strike. But this time I was on my feet. He didn't know much about stick fighting and his one idea was to bash in my skull. He struck down and hard. Blocking the downcoming blow with my forearm, I slid my right hand under and over his arm to grasp my own wrist in an arm lock. I had him and there was never much mercy in me. I just slammed the pressure to him and his hand opened and dropped the club as he screamed.

He went over backwards to the floor and I released him and let him fall. I had almost broken his arm. I could have without no trouble. He was game and he got up. When he tried to swing with his injured arm I was suddenly tired of the whole thing. I hit him four inches above the belt buckle with my left, and then clobbered him on the ear with my right. He went down, his ear split apart, gasping for breath.

"A man that can't fight shouldn't try," I commented. "He's just lucky I didn't break his fool neck."

Taking Pennywell by the elbow, I went to the door. "I'm taking this girl to a good home," I said, "but I'll be back."

Spud Tavis was slowly sitting up. "Tavis," I said, "you've got youngsters, Pennywell says. My advice is to go home an' take care of them. If you ever bother this young lady again, you'll answer to me. An' next time I won't play games."

The rain had wind behind it, lashing the boardwalk and the faces of the buildings. We slopped across to the livery stable, where I left Pennywell under the overhang and went in alone, gun in hand.

Nobody was there. I saddled up my horse, who looked almighty unhappy with me, and then mounted up. At the door I gave her a hand up and we went out and down the road. As we left I saw somebody standing on the edge of the walk, peering after me. Once out of sight and sound in the darkness we cut across a field, took a country lane, and headed for the mountains.

The trail began at a lightning-scarred pine and wound steeply up among the rocks, slick from rain and running water. After a climb of nearly half a mile we came to a huge boulder that hung over what was called a trail. It taken us nearly two hours to travel maybe a mile and a half of trail, and then we were riding smooth and in the woods a couple of thousand feet above the prairie.

Wet branches slapped at our faces and dripped water down our necks. Several times the horse slipped on the muddy trail. The horse I rode was bigger than most and powerful, but it was carrying double. After a while I got down and walked, leading the horse along.

"Logan Sackett," I said to myself, "you can get yourself into some mighty poor situations."

Here I was, slippin' an' sloppin' through a wet forest,

20

headin' toward what might be a bullet in my fat skull, and all because of some no-account drifter's girl.

The house when I saw it looked almighty big, even from up on the mountain. It looked the way folks figure a ha'nted house might look like, standin' up there on its hill, peerin' out over the country around.

Behind it there was a long building, more'n likely a bunkhouse. There were a couple of barns, sheds, and some corrals. I could see light reflected from a water tank. It must have been quite an outfit when it was all together an' workin' right.

We walked and slid down the steep hill behind the house, and lookin' back I could see why nobody tried that way in, because it was rimmed around with cliffs two or three hundred feet high or mountains too steep for a horse to climb.

I led my horse inside a barn and stripped off the saddle. The barn was empty and smelled like it'd been empty a long time. Very carefully we crossed to the bunkhouse and I opened the door, stepped in, and struck a match. It was empty, too. No bedrolls, nothing.

A few old dried-out, worn-out boots, some odds and ends of harness and rope, a dusty coat hung from a nail.

We crossed the yard and went very easily up the back steps. The door opened under my hand, and we stepped in.

All was dark and still. The house had the musty smell of a place long closed. Lightning flashed revealing a kitchen storeroom. We tiptoed on through it, opening the door into the kitchen.

There was a fire in the kitchen range, and the smell of warmth and coffee was in the room.

The floor creaked ever so slightly as we crossed it. I could feel the skin crawl on the back of my neck, but I laid a hand on that door.

By rights we should have had a gun barrel stuck in our

faces, but there hadn't been a sound. Was the old lady dead?

Gently I opened the door. Beyond was a big room, cavernous and dark. Lightning flashed and showed through the shuttered windows and the glass transom window over the door. And in that momentary flash I found myself looking across the room into the black muzzle of a big pistol. Behind it stood the old lady.

The flash, then darkness. "All right," her voice was steady, "I may be old but I have ears like a cat. If you so much as shift your feet I am going to fire, and mister, I can hit what I aim at."

"Yes, ma'am. I've a lady with me, ma'am."

"To the right of the door there is a lamp. There should still be a little coal oil in it. Take off the chimney, strike a match, and be mighty, mighty careful."

"Yes, ma'am. We're friendly, ma'am. We've just had a run-in with some folks down at the town."

Carefully I lifted off the lamp chimney, struck a match, and touched it to the wick. Then I replaced the chimney and the room was softly lit.

"Better stand clear of the light," she said quietly, "those no-accounts yonder shot two or three of them out for me."

"Yes, ma'am. My name is Logan Sackett, and this here girl is Pennywell Farman."

"Any kin to Deke Farman?"

"He was my father."

"Maybe he was a good father, but he was a shiftless, no-account cowhand. Never did earn his keep."

"That sounds like pa," Pennywell said mildly.

The hand that held the gun was steady as a rock. And it was no ordinary gun. It was one of those old-time Dragoon Colts that would blow a hole in a man big enough for your fist . . . or mine.

"What are you doin' here?" the old lady asked.

"Ma'am, this young lady taken on to cook an' care for

youngsters at the Tavis place. Spud Tavis made things bad for her, an' she run off an' fetched herself into town. She came to the Bon Ton huntin' the boss to ask for a job, and some of that crowd—Len Spivey for one—they talked kind of mean to her, ma'am. She needs a lady to set with, ma'am, and somebody who will teach her the things she should know. She's sixteen, and she's a good girl."

"Do you take me for a fool? Of course, she's a good girl. I can see that. What I want to know is what kind of a man are you? Are you fit company for her?"

"No, ma'am, I'm not. I'm mean, ma'am, meaner than a skunk, on'y I never figured to be comp'ny for her, only to bring her here. I'm fixin' to ride on, ma'am, soon's my horse is rested up."

"Ride on?" Her voice grew stronger. "Ride to where?"

"I don't rightly know, ma'am, just on. Just to ride on. I been a sight of places, worked at a whole lot of things. Was Milo Talon your son, ma'am?"

Suddenly the room was still. And then she said, "What do you know of Milo Talon?"

"Why, we met up down Chihuahua way, quite a spell back, only I understood his folks were all passed on."

"He was wrong, and I'm his ma. Where is Milo now?"

"Driftin', I reckon. We drifted together, there for a while, and got ourselves in a shootin' match down Laredo way."

"Milo was always a hand. He was quick to shoot."

"Yes, ma'am, or I'd be dead. He seen 'em sneakin' up on us before I did an' he cut loose. Yes, ma'am, Milo Talon could shoot. He had said his brother was better than him."

"Barnabas? At targets, maybe, or with a rifle, but Barnabas was never up to Milo when it came to hoedown-an'-scrabble shootin'."

There was silence in the room. "Ma'am? There's coffee settin' yonder. Mightn't we have some?"

23

She got up, placing the pistol in a worn holster slung from her hips. "What ever am I thinkin' of? Been so long since I had a guest I don't recall how to act. Of course, there's coffee."

She started toward the door, then paused. "Young man, would you mind taking a look out yonder? If you see anybody creepin' up . . . shoot him or her as the case might be."

She lighted the other lamp in the kitchen and then carried the lamp from the big front room back to join it.

"Nobody coming, ma'am. Looks like they're holed up against the rain."

"Fools! They might have had me. I fallen asleep in yonder. Heard the floor creak as you stepped into the kitchen or somewhere. They're a lazy lot. Gunslingers aren't what they used to be. Was a time you could hire *fighters*, but this lot that Flanner has are a mighty sorry bunch."

She turned, a tall old woman in a faded gray dress and a worn maroon sweater. She looked at me, then sniffed. "I might of knowed it. Clinch Mountain, ain't you?"

"What was that, ma'am?" I was startled.

"I said you're a Clinch Mountain Sackett, ain't you? I'd read your sign anywhere, boy. You're probably one of those no-account sons of Tarbil Sackett, ain't you?"

"Grandson, ma'am."

"I thought so. Knowed your folks, every durn last one of them, and a sorry lot they were, good for nothing but fightin' an' makin' moonshine whiskey."

"Are you from Tennessee, ma'am?"

"Tennessee? You're durned tootin', I am! I'm a Clinch Mountain Sackett myself! Married Talon an' came west an' we set up here. Fact is, a cousin of mine helped put this place together, and he was a Sackett. He went off somewhere in the mountains and never come back.

"Traipsin' just like you, he was, traipsin' after some

24

fool story of gold. Left some boys back in Tennessee, and a wife that was too good for him.

"Come in an' set, son, you're among home folks!"

3

It was comfortable in that old kitchen, and old as it was the place was neat as a man could wish. The floor was scrubbed and the copper pots shone brightly with light reflected by that coal-oil lamp.

The coffee smelled right good. Even though I'd had a cup at the Bon Ton down in town, this here was better, better by a whole lot.

"They said down in town you had you some hands," I told her.

She chuckled. "I aimed for them to think so. I been alone for nearly a year now. Bill Brock, he picked up some lead last time we had us a fight with those folks, and he died. I buried him out yonder." She nodded toward the area behind the house. "Figured to move him to a proper grave when the time came."

She taken a cup of coffee after she'd poured for us and then she came and set down. Her face was lined and old enough to have worn out two or three bodies but her eyes held fire. "You be Logan Sackett. Well, I d'clare! You a puncher?"

"I'm whatever it takes to get the coon," I said. "I guess I ain't much, Aunt Em. I'm too driven to driftin' an' gun play. Why, even that horse I'm ridin' yonder ain't mine. Come time to leave back yonder down the country I hadn't no time to buy a horse nor the money to do it with. This one was handy so I taken to his saddle and lit a shuck out of there."

She nodded. "I've seen it a time or two. Come daylight you go yonder to the barn an' turn that horse loose. He'll take time but he'll fetch up back home sooner or later. We've horses a-plenty here on the Empty."

"I wasn't figurin' on—"

"Don't you worry none. There's enough rooms in this here house for the whole of Grant's army, and then there's the bunkhouse. We ain't short of grub, although we could do with some fresh meat now and again.

"No reason you can't hole up here until the weather clears."

"Thank you, ma'am. On'y I was sort of figurin' on Californy. I been there a time or two and when winter comes I just naturally get chillblains. I thought maybe I'd head for Los Angeles, or maybe Frisco."

"I can pay," Aunt Em said. "You needn't worry none about that."

"I wouldn't take money from kinfolk. It's just that I—"

"Logan Sackett, you be still! You're not movin' a step until the weather shapes up. If you're worried about those folks out there, you just forget it. I can handle them, one at a time or all to onct."

"It ain't that, it's just that—"

"All right then, it's settled. I'll get you some blankets."

Looked to me like I wasn't going to see Californy for some time yet. That old lady just wasn't easy to talk to. She had her own mind and it was well made up ahead of time. Anyway, I was kind of curious to see what that outfit out front looked like.

"If I'm going to stay," I said, "I'll keep watch. You two go yonder and sleep."

When they had gone I got me a mattress off a bed in one of the rooms and laid it out on the floor, then I fetched blankets and settled in for the night.

Outside the rain beat down on the roof and walls of the old house, and the lightning flashed and flared, giving

26

a man a good view of what was happening at the gate and beyond. And that was just nothing.

The lamp was in the kitchen and I left it there, wanting no light behind me when I looked out. After watching for a while, I decided nobody was likely to make a move for a time, so I went back and stoked up the fire in the kitchen range and added a mite of water to the coffee so's there'd be a-plenty.

Off the living room there was a door opened into what must have been old Reed Talon's office. There were more books in there than I'd ever seen at one time in my life, and there were some sketches like of buildings and bridges, all with figures showing measurements written in. I couldn't make much of some of them, although others were plain enough. Studying those sketches made me wonder how a man would feel who built something like a bridge or a boat or a church or the like. It would be something to just stand back and look up at it and think he'd done it. Made a sight more sense than wandering around the country settin' up in the middle of a horse.

Time to time I catnapped. Sometimes I'd prowl a mite, and a couple of times I put on that slicker and went outside.

There was a wide porch on the house, roofed over, but with a good long parapet or wall that was four feet high. Talon had put loopholes in that wall a man could shoot from, and he'd built wisely and well.

When I came in I sat down with coffee, and then I heard those old shoes a-scufflin' and here come Em Talon.

"Well, Logan, it's good to see a Sackett again. It's been a good many years."

"I hear tell some of them have moved up around Shalako, out in western Colorado," I suggested. "Fact is, I know there's several out there. Cumberland Sacketts," I added, "good folks, too."

"The man who helped pa had some boys back in Tennessee. I often wonder what became of him." She filled her cup. "His oldest boy was named for William Tell."

"Met him. He's a good man, and he's sure enough hell on wheels with a six-shooter. No back-up to him."

"Never was back-up in no Sackett I can call to mind. I reckon there were some who lacked sand, but there's a rotten apple in every barrel."

She was a canny old woman, and we set there over coffee, with once in a while a look out to see if anybody was coming in on us. We talked of the Clinch Mountains, the Cumberland Gap country, and folks who'd moved west to hunt for land.

"Talon was a good man," she said. "I married well, if I do say it. When he first rode up to my gate I knowed he was the man for me, or none.

"All the Talons had a gift for working with their hands, they had the love of good wood in their fingers, an' when a Talon taken wood into his hands he felt of it like he loved it."

She looked over at me. "It's like you Sacketts with your guns."

"From what they tell me you're pretty good your own self."

"Had to be. Pa wasn't always home, and there were Injuns. I was never like some. Lots of folks lost relatives to Injuns, and hated 'em because. Me, I never did. They was just something else to contend against, like the storms, the stampedes, the drought, and the grasshoppers. A time or two I seen grasshoppers come in clouds that would darken the sun and strip bare the land like a plague." She stared off, as if calling up her memories.

"Shoot? Well, I guess yes. Gun loads was mighty scarce back yonder in the hills, and when somebody went out for meat for our family he or she was expected to come back with meat for every load taken."

She refilled my cup and hers. "Logan, I got to find Milo. This here place belongs to the boys, him and

28

Barnabas. I'm not so young as I used to be, an' one night I'll fall asleep and those out there, they'll close in an' finish me off. I need he'p, Logan."

I shifted in my chair, feeling guilty-like. I'd lost no ponies around here. Californy was where I'd be fixing to be, and then I had to put my oar into that squabble down in town.

"I could stay on a few days," I said. "There's nobody waitin' for me yonder. Or anywheres else," I added, thinking on it. I guess since my folks died nobody had ever waited on my coming or cared what happened.

"That Flanner," I said, "he carries a gun in a shoulder holster."

"He does? Well, I reckon he carries one someplace. He's killed a few. Nobody braces him." She looked up at me, real sharp. "You seen Johannes?"

"Not to know him. There were several men a settin' in the saloon. In the Bon Ton. But I don't know—"

"Wouldn't have been him. Johannes Duckett. He's some kin to Flanner, and he's not quite right in the head, I think. Or maybe he's just strange. But he's a dead shot with a gun of any kind and he's a back-shooter . . . he'll shoot you front, back, or sideways. Mostly he cares for the livery stable."

"I didn't see anybody."

"Well, he was around there, then. Whenever he ain't there, somebody else is, and when Johannes is about you just don't see him unless he's of a mind to let you."

After a time she went off to bed and I fussed around a mite, and taken a turn outside. Pretty soon Pennywell came down to spell me and I curled up on a mattress to take five.

Daylight was coming through the shutters when I awakened, and I could hear folks stirring around out in the kitchen. From the porch I could look over that layout there by the gate, and of a sudden I started gettin' sore.

Holding an old lady like that! And shooting at her so's she didn't dare stir out in front of her own house.

Setting there on the porch in the shadows I studied the layout and made up my mind that come sundown I was going to do some moving around of my own. California looked bright and pretty to me and I wasn't going to leave here with those fellers out there makin' trouble for Aunt Em.

Out back I fetched a bait of corn from the bin for my horse—I guess he'd never had it so good.

Em Talon was right. They had some mighty fine stock out yonder in the fenced pasture behind the barn, so I saddled up, roped myself a half dozen horses, and brought them up to the corral one at a time. Then I stripped the gear from the borrowed horse and turned it loose.

It ran off a ways, then commenced to graze out there betwixt those boys and the house. Finally as if it taken a notion to travel, it moved off.

Leaning on the corral I studied those horses. The ones I'd picked were mighty fine stock, all wearing the Empty brand. There was a tough-looking strawberry roan that I liked right off, and a steeldust gelding with a wise look about him.

Those were good horses but they hadn't been under a saddle for months, maybe. They'd take some riding, so I made up my mind to do it.

Whilst I was puttering around I got to studying on where Milo Talon might be. If I was to get shut of this job I'd better find him ... and that wasn't easy to do.

Milo was a man who covered country. There'd be folks in Brown's Hole might know where he was, or up in the Hole-in-the-Wall country. What I had to do was start the word moving along the trails. It might take time, but if Milo was alive, he'd hear it.

Meanwhile there was a lot to be done. I topped off those broncs, and they showed me plenty of action, but they were good stock. To make sure we'd have plenty of

30

riding stock in case of trouble, I topped off a few others, too.

The gate to the corral was sagging and a board on the back step had come loose, so I made out to fix them up. I never cared much for such work, liking to do nothing I couldn't do from a saddle, but it had to be done.

Working around, I gave the place some study. Old Talon, who had moved in here when the Injuns were on the warpath often as not, had built with cunning. And that was what had Flanner's boys in a bind . . . he'd built so there was no way he could be got at.

Moreover, each building was like a fort, and it was easy to move from one to the other without exposing yourself to rifle fire from the outside.

There are a lot of places in the mountains where small valleys or ravines open out into the plains. Talon had found such a place and built so that there was no access except right through his ranch. Which allowed him to control the grazing in a succession of small but pleasant valleys that cut deep into the mountains.

He had located most of the possibilities for trails into the area and had blasted rock to block them off, or had felled trees across them. It was a rugged area of deep canyons, rushing streams, and wild, broken ridges.

There isn't any place that I ever saw that couldn't be got into or out of, but often it isn't easy, and nobody wants to go scouting in rough country, scrambling up rock slides and the like when he is apt to get his skull opened up for trying.

Talon had been thinking about Injuns, I figure, but maybe he'd had the foresight to know that a lot of the savages wear store-bought clothes. Anyway, he was ready . . . else his widow would have been buried deep and this place would have been cut up and divided, or taken over by Flanner.

Meanwhile night was coming on. Just to see what would happen I taken a blanket on a stick and moved it in the shadows of the porch, standing well inside.

Sure enough, a rifle blasted and a bullet went right through that blanket. Now out where they were all they'd be able to see was something moving. They wouldn't know but what it was Em Talon.

Come evening time when the shadows are long and it begins to get hard to see, I taken my Winchester and went out through the kitchen.

Pennywell stopped me. "Where you going?"

Em turned from the stove. "I just fixed supper," she said, "you set down."

"Keep it warmed up. I'll be back." I hesitated in the back door. "Those boys out there can spread it around. I want to see what they do when it's all gathered up."

Outside I moved into the shadows. Nobody ever said no Clinch Mountain Sackett was anything but mean, and me and my brother Nolan, we shaped up to be the meanest. I never asked no favors and never gave none that I can recall, not when it came to fighting.

We Sackett boys had grown up among the Indians. Cherokees mostly, but we'd known and hunted with Creeks, Chickasaws, Choctaws, and Shawnees. What I done right then any one of those Injuns could have done, but I figure I did it as well as most. Anyway, I moved across that open ground, sort of filtering through the shadows, like.

There were three men settin' by that fire and I stood up and walked amongst them. I was right on them before they saw me and I kicked the boiling coffeepot into the lap of the nearest one.

The man whose back was to me started to get up and turn and I pushed him into the fire. Then I taken a swing with my rifle and fetched the next one in the belly. He went down and I walked into that outfit and never gave them a chance to get set.

Like I said, I'm a big man, but that ain't the important part. My shoulders and arms have beef on them from

32

wrassling broncs and steers, from swinging an ax and rafting logs down the Mississippi, and I was feeling no mercy for an outfit that would tackle an old woman.

The one I'd shoved into the fire jumped out of it and turned, grabbing for his six-shooter. Well, if he wanted to play that way he could. I just pointed my rifle at him, which I held only in my right hand, and let him have the big one right through the third button on his shirt. If he ever figured to sew that particular button on again he was going to have a scrape it off his backbone . . . if he had any.

The man into whose lap I'd kicked the coffeepot had troubles enough. He was jumping around like mad and I could see I'd ruined his social life for some time to come. He'd been scalded real good and he wasn't going to ride anywhere, not anywhere at all.

The other one was on his hands and knees, gasping and groaning. I pushed him over on his back with my boot and put the rifle in his face and looked down the barrel at him.

"You ever been to Wyoming?" I asked him. "Or Montana?"

He stared at me, his face a sickly yellow like his insides must have been.

"Well, when you can get on your feet, you start for one or the other, and you keep going. If I ever see you around again I ain't going to like it."

Taking up the three rifles I busted them over the nearest rock, then threw the rest of them into the fire along with the ammunition and their tent.

Then I sort of backed off into the night and went back to the house.

Aunt Em an' Pennywell, they were on the porch watching the fire out there, and when I came up the steps I said, "You kep' my supper warm, ma'am?"

"Yes, I did. Dish it up, Pennywell."

When I sat down to table, Aunt Em she said nothing

at all, but Pennywell was younger and almighty curious. "What happened out there? What did you do?"

"Like Samson," I said, "I went among the Philistines and smote them, hip and thigh." And after a good swallow of coffee, I grinned at her and said, "And one of them in the belly."

4

The rain soaked up the ground and went on about its business, and the sun came out hot as roasting ears. When I looked out front there was nothing beyond the gate but a lot of distance. Flanner's boys had taken out, and I didn't look for them to come back.

There was work to be done around the place. No Clinch Mountain Sackett was much account at fixin' up. Our places yonder in the high-up hills always looked fit to fall apart, only they never done it. Still, it griped my innards to see such a fine place run down like it was. Besides, I was wishful to be handy if any of Flanner's outfit came back again.

After a day or two, and no trouble showing, I taken off to the meadows to find us some meat.

Each meadow was a mite higher than the last, and all told there was a thousand acres of good bottom land, the stream running from one to the other. There was a fair stand of grazing under the scattered trees that stretched back to the mountains from the edge of the meadows, stretching back to sheer walls that reminded me of the Hermosa Cliffs edging the Animas Valley near Durango.

Old Man Talon had known what he was about when he came to this place. He had water, grass and shade, hay and timber for the cutting. There were other, higher meadows, bordered with groves of aspen. He had what was needed, logs for building and shelter from the worst of the storms. Above all, he had a closed-in land where few cowhands were needed, and where he could cut hay on the meadows against the cold of winter.

Below the ranch lay thousands of acres of prairie completely dependent for water on his mountain land. That prairie would graze a lot of cattle, but all those vast acres were nothing but useless without water for stock. Who held the Empty held the range. No question about it.

At first I paid no mind to hunting. From time to time I glimpsed deer but passed them by to scout the country. Nowhere did I see any fresh sign of horse or man, and that was what I hunted, being doubtful of any ranch a man couldn't get into.

There are few things men cannot do if they have a mind to, and I had a hunch Flanner had been trying the easy way. Now he would have to come up with something else, and that was what we must be ready for. Meanwhile, riding and looking, I corraled myself into a patch of thinking.

Milo Talon was a far-riding man, and he'd be somewhere along the outlaw trail. He favored no country over another, but moved. He was a more slender man than me, lean and hard as seasoned timber, good with horse, rope, or gun, and a handsome devil to boot.

Brown's Hole stuck in my mind, and it wasn't far off. If he wasn't there it was certainly a place where a man could start the word along the wild country trails. And if I was to get shut of this place I'd have to get him over here.

Barnabas? He was supposed to be in France. I knew nothing about France or any other place I couldn't get to on a horse.

Flanner wanted this outfit and he could buy the men to take it for him. A man who wouldn't hesitate to get an old woman killed was a man who wouldn't stop at much a body could think of. If he kept on pushing he was going to make me sore as a grizzly with a bad tooth, and I didn't want that. When I get really down to gravel mad I act up something fierce, and I had enough posses hunting me here and yon as it was.

A man could live well off the country. Deer and elk were around and I'd seen a sign of bear and lion. A mountain lion swings a big circle—maybe thirty-odd miles of it—and he usually manages to live off the elk or deer that are getting on in years or are too young to escape. From time to time he takes a rancher's calf.

Living in wild country you become like one of the animals. You learn their ways, you kill what you need to live and you bother none of the others and fight shy of them. I never killed anything unless pushed to it . . . including men.

Clinch Mountain, yonder in Tennessee, was mighty sparse on topsoil, at least where we Sacketts lived. It made up for beauty what it lacked in richness. Ma used to say it offered more food for the soul than for the belly, so we Sackett boys taken to making our living with rifle and trap, but we never figured to take more than our due. We trapped a stream a year or two, then held off, let it be, and worked another one to let the first recover. There was a lot we boys didn't know, with no schoolin' to speak of, but we learned early that if you want water on the land you need beaver in the high country. They build their dams, keep them in repair, and they hold back in ponds water that would run off down the country to the sea. I never seen the sea, but they tell me it's off down the country somewheres.

Pa told us we held the land in trust. We were free to use it so long as it was kept in shape for the generations following after, for our sons and yours.

This was rugged country, faulted and twisted. It looked like it had been crumpled like a shoot of thin paper, with tilted layers whose saw-toothed edges had been honed down some by wind and rain. It would take months to learn all the canyons and hollows, rising higher and higher into green forest and finally to timberline and the gray and lonely peaks up yonder against the sky.

I'm tellin' you, man, that there was *country!*

The stock I'd seen was in good shape in spite of the fact they'd been kept in the high country, pasture Talon probably held back for the hot weather. Ordinarily up to this time they'd have been down on the flat plains, but due to the shennanigans of Flanner's boys they had to be holed up in the hills, which meant scant feed for later in the year.

On the way back I killed me a deer, dressed and skinned it, then rode on to the ranch.

When I got there Aunt Em was already looking rested. Pennywell was pert, kind of flirty when she looked my way, but I fought shy of her. She bit her lips every time she turned her back to make them redder, and I'd seen her pinching her cheeks to bring the color to them. Not that she needed it much.

If she was setting her cap for me she was wastin' time. I'm too old a coon to be caught by the first trap I see, and I'd baited too many traps myself not to recognize the signs.

We set up to table and it was fine cookin', mighty fine. I said as much and Em said Pennywell done it, so I knew they were in it together. No wet-behind-the-ears girl could put vittles like that together.

Mostly when a girl invites a man to supper her sister or her mother or some friend fix up the meal, and all she does is put on a fussy little postage-stamp apron and set the table and dish it up just like she'd done it all herself.

By the hour I was gettin' irritated. I could have been into Arizona, almost, by this time, and headed for Californy and that ocean-sea. I was out there before, but never got right where I could see it. This time it would be different.

There was nothing out there but silence and the empty prairie, but I wanted them to come. I wanted them to come so's I could have it done with and be gone.

I never was much on waiting unless it was for game. I get meaner and meaner as time goes on. And I don't like being corraled. It just don't set right.

Which brought me around to thinking of Brown's Hole. Brown's Hole was a colossal big hollow set down amongst the mountains with mighty few ways to get in or out. It was a trapper's rendezvous one time, then mostly an outlaw hangout, although a few cattlemen had wintered herds there.

There were a few horse and cattle thieves who holed up between runnin' off one man's stock and another's. Tip Gault was there. For an outlaw he was a decent sort and a man I respected. I couldn't say the same for Mexican Joe. Mexicans and me usually got along. I'd spent some time down Sonora way, and they raised some of the best riders and ropers you'll find anywhere, and some mighty fine folks. But Mexican Joe was another sort of hombre entirely. The way I heard it he'd been run out of Mexico for things he'd done, but he was a mighty mean man with either gun or knife, favoring the latter.

I'd seen him a time or two, and he'd seen me, but so far we'd never locked horns.

What I had to do was make a fast ride to the Hole and back, trying to get out without Flanner knowing I was gone, and then get back before he found out. Anybody in the Hole might know where Milo was, but the ones most likely to know or to pass the word along were Tip Gault or Isom Dart.

Gault's outfit rustled horses and cattle mostly. It was not much of a business with them. They were just out to get money enough to throw a wingding once in awhile and have eating money.

Dart was a horse thief, too, but more cautious. He'd come close to losing his hair or winding up at the end of a rope not long before and he was a cautious man. That first close shave had taught him a lesson. He'd been a slave, freed by the war, and had come west under another name. He knew everybody along the outlaw trail and would give the word to any drifter who came along. Wherever Milo Talon was, he'd hear that word sooner or later. I hoped it would be sooner. What I really hoped was that Milo would be wintering in the Hole from time to time and they might know where he'd gone.

"Aunt Em," I said, when supper was finished, "I got to ride off a ways."

"Are you pullin' your stakes?"

"No, ma'am, but we got to get word to your son. I think if I rode out of here a spell I could give the word to a man who would pass it along."

She looked up at me, Em did. That old woman was no fool; she'd lived close to the edge for a good long time and she knew things.

"You going into the Hole?"

"Well . . ." I hesitated, not wanting to lie, "I guess that's the best grapevine in the world, out of there."

"You mean Isom Dart? You tell him you're a friend of mine. We saw him through it once when he was bad hurt."

"Flanner's cookin' up something, and I hate to pull out like this, but it's got to be done."

We talked it around over coffee, thinking over the trail I had to ride. Aunt Em had been in the Hole herself, with her husband when they first came west.

"We wintered in there our ownselves," she said. "We'd heard of it from some Cherokees who held cattle there."

Pennywell hadn't much to say. She sat across the table looking big-eyed at me and making me uneasy. When a talking woman sits quiet a man had better look at his hole card and keep a horse saddled.

The old house was warm and quiet. Taking up a rifle I walked out the back door and around to the front, holding close to the wall. Nothing showed against the skyline, but probably they wouldn't, anyway.

I stood listening for a while, but the sounds seemed right and I went back to the stable, forked down some hay for the stock, and looked over the horses. Then I went to the bunkhouse and got a pair of old, wore-out boots somebody had cast off. I taken them to the house.

"Ma'am," I said to Pennywell, "I want you to put these on."

She looked at the boots and then at me. "They're too big," she said, "and too old. Besides, I've got shoes."

"You've got none that make man tracks, and that's what I want."

She put on the boots and we walked out to the gate and up where the Flanner gunmen had their camp. We walked around, leaving tracks. They'd figure mine were the big ones, but they'd surely figure there was at least one more man on the place.

Later that night I got moccasins out of my saddlebags, put them on, and went out again. That way they'd see those tracks, too.

We Sacketts were mountain folk, and that meant we'd been woodsmen before we were riders. All of us had growed up among Indians and had learned to like moccasins for work in timber country; a man can feel a dry stick under his foot and not step down on it with a moccasin. With a boot or shoe it isn't that easy to go quiet.

Time was wasting, so when I came back I turned in for an hour or two of sleep. When I woke up, I got dressed and went into the kitchen.

Em Talon was there, and there was hot coffee on the stove. "I figured you'd be riding," she said. "Nothing like coffee to set a man on the right trail."

"Thanks," I said. I taken the coffee and set down

across that well-washed kitchen table. "Aunt Em, you're quite a woman."

"Always wanted to be six feet high," she said, "my brothers were all six-footers, and I aimed to be high as them. I never quite made it."

"You stand tall in any outfit," I said. "I'd like to have known your husband."

"Talon was a man . . . all man. He walked strong and he thought right, and no man ever left his door hungry, Indian, black man, or white. Nor did he ever take water for any man."

"He was a judge of land," I said, "and of women."

"We had it good together," Em said quietly, "we walked a quiet way, the two of us, and never had to say much about it to one another."

She paused. "I just looked at him and he looked at me and we knew how it was with each other."

Hours later, well down the trail to Brown's Hole, I remembered that. Well, they'd been lucky. It was not likely I'd ever find a woman like that, but no matter what any man says, there's nothing better than two, a man and woman, who walk together. When they walk right together there's no way too long, no night too dark.

5

The Union Pacific tracks lay to the north, and beyond was the Overland Trail to California. On the Pacific side of South Pass that route divided into two, the northern becoming the trail to Oregon.

Horse and cattle thieves operating out of Brown's Hole

had developed a thriving business stealing stock from emigrants on one trail and selling to those on the other. Occasionally the thieves drove their stolen stock into Brown's Hole for sale the following season. The grass was good, and by comparison with the country around the winters were mild.

To the north and east lay the Hole-in-the-Wall country; north and west from there, the Crazy Mountains with the border of Canada beyond. To the southwest of Brown's Hole lay Utah's San Rafael Swell with its Robbers' Roost, and south of that, Horse Thief Valley near Prescott, and a ranch near Alma, New Mexico. This was the country of the so-called Outlaw Trail.

In fact it was a maze of trails, obvious and hidden, and along those trails ranchers or homesteaders were friendly to drifting men, asking no questions, and providing no information to strangers.

Originally most of the trails had been scouted by Indians or mountain men, and here and there they had located hideouts away from prying eyes. A drifting man might ride from the Mexican border to Canada and be assured of meals and shelter or an exchange of horses anywhere along the route.

Those who rode the outlaw trail were not all wanted men; some were tough cowhands or drifters who traveled with the seasons and had friends among the wild bunch. A few were occasional outlaws, rustling a few cows when the occasion offered, playing it straight the rest of the time.

Milo Talon was known along the Trail. As there was constant movement up and back, it seemed the best way to get in touch with him was just to ride to the Hole and pass the word.

Morning came with me a-horseback. By daylight I'd put the Empty far behind and was snaking along a trail up through the pines and skirting the aspen groves. It was a fine, clear morning with the air washed clean by rain and drops hanging silver on every leaf. Even the wild things a body saw didn't seem to mind him much, so pleased they were with the morning.

My horse and me were of a mind. We taken our time, just breathing the good air, keeping an eye out for trouble, but just enjoying it. Far off and below I seen a dot that had to be buffalo. Most of them had been killed off, but here and there small herds had taken to the mountain valleys. Maybe two hundred in the lot I saw.

Of a sudden I rode out on a grassy slope that dropped steeply off into a valley far, far below. Ahead of me and a mite higher was a thick stand of aspen, and turning my horse I skirted the edge of that grove until I came on a likely spot. Putting my horse on a picket rope, I bunched a few sticks and with some shredded bark and twigs built myself a coffee-making fire.

I'd backed up against that grove on purpose. Looked at from down below no smoke would show against the white of the tree trunks and the gray-green of the leaves. From alongside the aspen a little branch trickled down over the rocks, twisting and turning to find itself a way down the mountain. It was so narrow in places the grass almost covered it from view. Dipping up a pot of water I set her on the fire, dumped in some coffee, and waited for it to boil. With that, some jerky and a chunk of homemade bread I figured to make do.

There's no prettier place than a stand of aspen. The elk and beaver like the bitter inner bark, and you'll nearly always find them where there's aspen. There's no thing that provides more grub for wildlife than the aspen grove.

There's usually wood around. The aspen is self-pruning, and as it grows taller it sheds its lower branches, just naturally reaching for the sun. Those branches dry out quickly and make excellent kindling.

Much as I wished to be back at the ranch for the safety of the womenfolks, I didn't figure to lose my hair in the process. Stopping to make coffee was giving my horse a rest, giving me food to start a long day, but it was also giving me time to watch my back trail a little.

I was pretty sure I'd come away from the Empty without being seen, but a man can get killed taking things for granted. If anybody was on my trail I wanted to look him—or her—over before they came up to me.

Meanwhile, setting there in the morning sun and watching my water get hot was a pleasure I could take to heart. I never was one for rushing through a country. I like to take my time, breathe the air, get the feel of it . . . I like to smell it, taste it, get it located in my brain.

The thing to remember when traveling is that the trail is the thing, not the end of the trail. Travel too fast and you miss all you are traveling for.

When my coffee was boiled good and black I poured myself a cup. It was strong—take the hide off a bull, that stuff would. Fellow I punched cows with down Sonora way said my coffee was dehorning fluid . . . one drop and a bull's horns would melt right off.

It ain't true, but it does measure up. A cup of it will open a man's eyes.

Chewing some jerky, I tasted that coffee now and again, and kept an ear out for sound and one eye on my horse. That horse was wild and a wild horse has all the senses of a deer and a good deal more savvy.

Pretty soon the roan lifted his head, pricked up his ears, and spread his nostrils. I forked my Winchester around and slipped the thong of the butt of my pistol. I wasn't one to hunt trouble, although I've buried a few who did.

There were two of them, studying the trail as they rode, and they had not seen me. Holding the Winchester in my hands, I stood up slowly. At that instant my horse whinnied and their heads turned sharply as if on one neck.

"Lookin' for something, boys?" My Winchester was easy

in my hands. I never sight a gun of any kind; I just look where I'm shooting.

They didn't like it very much. They were tough-looking characters, and both of them rode Eight-Ladder-Eight brands on their horses. Their horses were Morgans, fine stock, and the brands were a rewrite job if I ever saw one.

"Eight-Ladder-Eight," I commented sarcastically, "an' Morgan horses. Ain't many Morgans in this part of the country, boys, but a good man with a cinch ring and a hot fire could change a Six-Four-Six into an Eight-Ladder-Eight without half trying."

"You saying we stole these horses?"

"You did or somebody did," I said, "But if I were you boys I'd get shut of them, an' quick."

"Why?" one of them said.

"You ever heard of Dutch Brannenburg?"

"Wasn't he the one who chased those hombres from Montana to Texas?"

"Uh-huh. That's the one." I grinned at them. "You boys maybe don't know it, but he's registered a Six-Four-Six brand. You're sittin' right up in the middle of two of his horses."

Seemed to me their faces turned a shade gray under the tan. "You're funnin'," one of them said. "Why, we—!"

"Shut up, you damn' fool!" The older man was as sore as he was scared. "I tol' you it looked too damn' easy!"

"He's probably right behind you now," I told them, "and from what I hear of Dutch he wastes no time. You boys better learn to pray while you're ridin'. Dutch takes pride in his horses."

They headed off down the trail, rattling their hocks out of there. Me, I finished my coffee, tightened my cinch, and was just about to step into the leather when I heard them coming.

Dutch was a tough man. He was maybe fifty years old and nearly as wide as he was tall, and every ounce of

45

him was rawhide and iron. There were nine in the party and they swept up there just as I turned. My Winchester was still in my hands.

They taken a quick look at me and at my horse. "You there!" Dutch shouted. "Did you see a couple of men ride through here?"

"I wasn't looking very close," I said.

He pushed his horse at me. He was square-jawed and mean. I'd heard a lot about Dutch and liked none of it. He ranched, but he ranched like he was bull of the woods. You crossed him and you died . . . I'd heard he'd set fire to a couple of rustlers he'd caught.

"You'd have been a lot smarter if you'd given me a straight answer. I think you're one of them."

"You're a damned liar," I said. "You don't think any such thing."

He started to grab iron but that Winchester had him covered right where he lived.

"You boys sit tight," I told the others. "If one of you makes a wrong move I'm going to kill your boss."

"You ain't got the guts," he said, his tone ugly. "Kill him, boys."

"Boss," a slim, wiry man was talking, "that's Logan Sackett."

A bad reputation can get a man in a lot of trouble, but once in a while it can be a help. Dutch Brannenburg sort of eased back in his saddle and I saw his tongue touch his lips. Dry, I reckon.

"You know the tracks of your own horses," I said, "and you can read sign. So don't try to swing too wide a loop. Your hide punctures the same as any man's."

He reined his horse around. "You watch yourself, Sackett," he said. "I don't like you."

"I'll watch," I said, "and when you come after my hide, you'd better hide behind more men."

He swung his horse around and swore, muttering in a

low, vicious tone. "I don't need any men, Sackett. I can take you myself . . . any time."

"I'm here," I said.

"Boss?" That slim man's voice was pleading. "Those thieves are gettin' away, boss."

He swung his horse back to the trail. "So they are," he said sharply, and led off down the trail.

That was a mean man, I told myself, and a man to watch. I'd crossed him, backed him down, made him look less than he liked to look in front of his men.

"Logan," I said, "you've made you an enemy." Well, here and yonder I had a few. Maybe I could stand one more.

Nevertheless, I made myself a resolution to get nowhere near Dutch Brannenburg. Then or ever.

He had come west like many another pioneer and had taken up land where it meant a fight to hold it. Trouble was, after he'd used force a few times to hold his own against enemies it became a way of life to him. He liked being known as a hard, ruthless man. He liked being known as a driver. He had earned his land and earned his way, but now he was pushing, walking hard-shouldered against the world. He had begun in the right, but he had come to believe that because he did it, whatever he did, it was right to do. He made his own decisions as to who was criminal and who was not, and along with the horse and cow thieves he had wiped out a few innocent nesters and at least one drifting cowhand.

I'd been on the way and in the way, and only my own alertness had kept me alive. Now I'd made him stand back and he would not forgive.

The trail I'd followed had lost whatever appeal it had, so I mounted up and rode up the mountain, skirting the aspen and weaving my way through the scattered spruce that lay beyond. Somewhere up ahead was an old Indian trail that followed along the acres of the mountains above timberline. I was gambling Brannenburg did not know it.

His place was down in the flat land, and I had an idea he wasn't the type to ride the mountains unless it was demanded of him or unless he was hunting somebody.

The trail was there, a mere thread winding its way through a soggy green meadow scattered with fifty varieties of wild flowers, red, yellow, and blue.

Twice I saw deer . . . a dozen of them in one bunch, and on a far-off slope, several elk. There were marmots around all the while and a big eagle who kept me company for half the morning. I never did decide whether he was hoping I'd kill something he could share or if he was just lonely.

The peaks around me were ragged and gray, bare rock clean of snow except for a patch here and there in a shady place. Nor was there sound but that from the hoofs of my horse on the soft earth or occasionally glancing off a bit of rock.

It was the kind of trail I had ridden many times, and as on other times I rode with caution. A lonely trail it was, abandoned long since by the Indians who made it, but no doubt their ghosts were still walking along these mountainsides, through these same grasses.

Once I saw a silver-tip grizzly in the brush at the edge of the timber. He stood up to get a better view of me, a huge beast, probably weighing half a ton or more, but he was a hundred yards off and unafraid. My horse snorted and shied a bit, but continued on.

There were lion tracks in the trail. They always take the easiest way, even here where there are few obstructions. I'd not get a sight of the lion—they know the man smell and edge away from it.

It was mid-afternoon before I stopped again. I found a stream of snow water running off the ridge and an abandoned log cabin built by some prospector. There was a tunnel on the mountainside, and a pack rat had been in the cabin, but nobody else had been there for a long time.

I drank from the stream and left the cabin alone, not caring to be trapped inside a building, the first place anyone would look. I went back in a little cluster of pines and built my fire where the smoke would be dissipated by the evergreen branches above.

The coffee tasted good. I ate some more of the bread and chewed some jerky while drinking it, and I watched the trail below and the valley opening into the mountains, smoky with distance.

Two days later I rode into Brown's Hole from the east.

The Hole is maybe thirty-three or four miles long by five to six miles wide, watered by the Green River and a few creeks that tumble down off Diamond Mountain or one of the others to end up in the Green. It is sagebrush country, with some timber on the mountains and cedar along the ridges.

The man I was looking for was Isom Dart . . . at least that was the name he was using. His real name had been Huddleston . . . Ned, I think. He was a black man, and he had ridden with Tip Gault's outfit until riders from the Hat put them out of business.

I planned to stop at Mexican Joe Herrara's cabin on Vermilion Creek. Riding into the Hole I had come on a man driving some cows. When I asked about Dart, he looked me over careful-like and then said I might find him at Herrara's cabin, but to be careful. If Mexican Joe got mad at me and started sharpening his knife, I would be in trouble.

I was hunting trouble, but as for Joe, I'd heard about him before and I didn't much care whether he got mad or not.

There didn't seem to be anyone about when I got to the cabin. I pulled up and stepped down.

6

As I tied my horse to the corral with a slipknot, I kept an eye on the cabin. Men of that stamp would surely have heard me come up, and right now they were undoubtedly sizing me up.

In those days no law ever rode into the Hole. Most law around the country didn't even know where it was or just how to get in, and they'd find little to welcome them, although a few honest cattlemen like the Hoy outfit were already there.

Hitching my gun belt into a comfortable position, I walked up to the door.

As I came up on the rock slab that passed for a stoop the door opened suddenly and a Mexican was standing there. He wasn't Herrara, not big enough or mean enough.

"Buenos días, amigo," I said. "is the coffee on?"

He looked at me a moment, then stepped aside. There were three men in the cabin when I stepped in. I spotted Herrara at once, a tall, fierce-looking Mexican, not too dark. Sitting at the table with him was a white man who had obviously been drinking too much. He looked soft, not like a rider. There was another Mexican squatting on his heels in the corner.

"Passin' through," I commented, "figured you might have coffee."

Nobody spoke for a minute; Herrara just stared at me, his black eyes unblinking. Finally, the Anglo said, "There's coffee, and some beans, if you'd like. May I help you?"

He went to the stove in the corner and picked up the pot, filling a cup for me. Pulling back a chair, I sat down. The big white man brought me the coffee and a dish of beef and beans.

"Has Dutch Brannenburg been through?"

Herrara stared at me. "You ride for Dutch?"

I laughed. "Him an' me don't see eye to eye. I met him yonder and we had words. He's headed this way, hunting two horse thieves . . . Anglos," I added, "but he hangs whoever he finds."

"He did not hang you," Herrara said, still staring.

"I didn't favor the idea. The situation being what it was, he figured he could wait."

"The situation?" the Anglo asked.

"My Winchester was sort of headed his way. His motion was overruled, as they'd say in a court of law."

"He is coming this way?"

"There's nine of them," I said, "and they size up like fighters."

For a minute or two nobody said anything, and then around a mouthful of beans and beef, I said, "They'll come in from the north, I'm thinking. I didn't find any tracks in the Limestone Ridge country."

They all looked at me. "You came that way?"

I shrugged. "Joe," I said, "I'd been in this Hole two, three times before you left South Pass City."

He didn't like that very much. Mexican Joe had killed a man or two over that way and they'd made it hot for him, so he'd pulled his stakes.

I'd come in there first as a long-geared apple-knocking youngster. I'd been swinging a hammer on the U.P. tracks and got into a shooting at the End of Track. The men I killed had friends and I had none but a few Irish track-workers who weren't gunfighters, so I pulled my freight.

"Are you on the dodge?" It was the Anglo who asked the question.

"Well," I said, "there's a posse from Nebraska that's probably started back home by now. I came thisaway because I figured I'd see Isom Dart . . . I wanted to sort of pass word down the trail."

"What word?" Herrara's tone was belligerent.

The Mexican had been drinking wine, as had the others. He was in an ugly mood and I was a stranger who did not seem impressed by him. There had been some other Mexicans down in Sonora and Chihuahua who weren't impressed, either, and that was why he was up here.

"Milo Talon," I said, "is a friend of mine, and I want to pass the word along that he's needed on the Empty, over east of here, and that he's to come careful."

"I'll tell Dart," the American said.

Herrara never took his eyes off me. He was mean, I knew that, and he'd cut up several men with his knife. He had a way of taking it out and honing it until sharp, then with a yell he'd jump you and start cutting. But the honing act was to get a man scared before he jumped him. It was a good stunt, and usually it worked.

He got out his whetstone, but before he could draw his knife I drew mine. "Say, just what I need." Before he knew what I was going to do I had reached over and taken the stone. Then I began whetting my own blade.

Well, it was a thing to see. He was astonished, then mad. He sat there empty-handed while I calmly put an edge to my blade, which was already razor sharp. I tried the blade on a hair from my head and it cut nicely, so I passed the stone back to him.

"Gracias," I said, smiling friendly-like. "A man never knows when he'll need a good edge."

My knife was a sort of modified Bowie, but made by the Tinker. No better knives were ever made than those made by the Tinker back in Tennessee. He was a Gypsy pack peddler who drifted down the mountains now and again, but he sold mighty few knives. The secret of those blades had come from India where his people, thousands of years back, had been making the finest steel in the world. The steel for the fine blades of Damascus and Toledo actually came from India, and there's an iron pillar in India that's stood for near two thousand years, and not a sign of rust.

I showed them the knife. "That there," I said, "is a Tinker-made knife. It will cut right through most blades and will cut a man shoulder to belt with one stroke."

Tucking it back in my belt, I got up. "Thanks for the grub. I'll be drifting. I don't figure to be trapped inside if Dutch comes along."

Nobody said a word as I went outside, tightened my cinch, and prepared to mount.

Then the American came out. "That was beautiful," he said, "Joe is an old friend of mine, but he's had that coming for a long time. He didn't know what to think. He still doesn't."

"You're an educated man," I said.

"Yes. I studied law."

"There's need for lawyers," I said. "I may need one myself sometime."

He shrugged, then looked away. "I should pull out," he said. "I just sort of drifted into this, and I've stayed on. I guess it doesn't make much sense."

"If I knew the law," I said, "I'd hang out my shingle. This is a new country. No telling where a man might go."

"I guess you're right. God knows I've thought of it, but sometimes a man gets caught in a sort of backwater."

I stepped into the saddle, listening beyond his voice. Nobody came from the cabin. I heard no sound on the trail.

The American pointed. "Isom Dart has a cabin down that way. He's a black man, and smart."

"We've met," I said.

He looked up at me. "They'll be wondering who you are," he said. "It isn't often a man stands up to Mexican Joe."

"The name is Sackett . . . Logan Sackett," I said and rode off. When I looked back he was still looking after me, but then he turned and walked toward the cabin door.

I trusted the Anglo. I had heard of him before, and he was a man of much education who seemed to care for nothing but sitting in the cabin and drinking or talking with the Mexicans or passers-by.

This Brown's Hole was a secret place, although the Indians had known of it. Ringed with hills, some of them that could not be passed, it was a good place, too, a good place for men like me. There were places like this in Tennessee where I had been born, but they were more green, lovelier and not so large.

My thoughts returned to Emily Talon. She was a Sackett. She was my kin and so deserving of my help. Ours was an old family, with old, old family feelings. Long ago we had come from England and Wales, but the family feeling within us was older still, old as the ancient Celtic clans I'd heard spoken of. It was something deep in the grain, but something that should belong to all families . . . everywhere. I did not envy those who lacked it.

There'd never been much occasion to think on it. When trouble fetched around the corner we just naturally lit in and helped out. Mostly, we could handle what trouble came our way without help, but there was a time or two, like that time down in the Tonto Basin country when they had Tell backed into a corner.

Riding through wild country leaves a man's mind free to roam around, and while a body never dast forget what he's doing, one part of his mind keeps watch while another sort of wanders around. My thoughts kept returning to Em Talon and the Empty.

That old woman was alone except for a slip of a girl, and you could bet Jake Flanner was studying ways to get her away from the ranch. Chances were he thought I was still around, but if he did know I was gone he'd figure I was gone for good.

Well, if I could find Milo Talon, I would be.

Right now I wanted Milo more'n anybody, but I hadn't any fancy ideas about being safe in Brown's Hole. So far most of the folks in the Hole, if they weren't outlaws themselves at least tolerated them. The Hoys, however, tolerated them least of all, as they'd lost some stock from time to time.

From time to time I rode off the trail and waited in the cedars to study my back trail, and I kept my eyes on the tracks. I wanted to see Dart, but there were others around I'd no desire to see at all.

Suddenly I heard hoofs a-coming and I pulled off the trail. It was Dart, and he was riding a sorrel gelding. They called Isom Dart a black man and he'd been a slave, but he surely wasn't very black.

He seen me as quick as I did him. "H'lo, Logan. What you all a-doin' up thisaways?"

"Huntin' you. I want to pass word to Milo Talon. He's needed on the Empty. His ma's still alive and she's in trouble. He's to come in careful . . . and anybody in town is likely an enemy."

Dart nodded. "You know how 'tis, Logan. He's a fast-ridin' man, and he may be a thousand mile from here. I'll get word to him."

I gathered my reins. "You'd better hole up for a while your ownself. Brannenburg is huntin' rustlers."

"I never been in his neck o' the woods."

"Don't make no dif'rence. Dutch thinks he's godaw-mighty these days. If you ain't a banker or a big cattle-man you're a cow thief."

No man in his right mind rides the same trail going back, not if he has enemies or it's Injun country. After leaving Dart I taken to the water, swam the Green and edged along through the brush, weaving a fancy trail for

55

anybody wishful of hunting me. I backtracked several times, rode over my own trail, swam the Green again, and stayed in the water close to the bank for a ways.

When I did come out of the water I was in a thick stand of cedar and I worked my way east toward the Limestone Ridge. Turning, I walked my horse toward the gap that led to Irish Canyon, then turned east again and crossed Vermilion Creek and proceeded on east to West Boone Draw.

Most of the time I was riding in cedar or brush or following draws so that I could keep out of sight. I saw nobody, heard nothing, yet I had a spooky feeling.

There are times riding in the hills when you know you are alone and yet you are sure you are watched. Sometimes I think the ghosts of the old ones, the ones who came before the Indians, sometimes I think they still follow the old trails, sit under the ancient trees, or listen to the wind in the high places, for surely not even paradise could be more lonely, more beautiful, more grand than the high peaks of the San Juans or the Tetons or this land through which I rode.

There's more of me in the granite shoulders of the mountain or in the trunks of the gnarled cedars than there is in other men. Ma always said I was made to be a loner, and Nolan like me. We were twins, him and me, but once we moved we rode our separate ways and never seemed to come together again, nor want to. There'd been no bad feeling between us, it was as if we sensed that one of us was enough at one time in one place.

Riding out of the brush I looked across the country toward East Boone Draw. I just sat there for a while, feeling the country and not liking what I felt.

There was something spooky about Brown's Hole. Maybe it was that I couldn't get Brannenburg out of my mind. The Dutchman was hard . . . he was stone. His brain was eroded granite where the few ideas he had carved deep their ruts of opinion. There was no way for another

56

idea to seep in, no place for imagination, no place for dreams, none for compassion or mercy or even fear.

He knew no shadings of emotion, he knew no half-rights or half-wrongs or pity or excuse, nor had he any sense of pardon. The more I thought of him the more I knew he was not evil in himself, and he would have been shocked that anybody thought of him as evil. Shocked for a moment only, then he'd have shut the idea from his mind as nonsense. For the deepest groove worn into that granite brain was the one of his own rightness.

And that scared me.

A man like that can be dangerous, and it made me uneasy to be riding in the same country with him. Maybe it was that I'd a sense of guilt around him and he smelled it.

Here and there I'd run off a few cattle from the big outfits. They branded anything they found running free without a brand, but let a nester or cowhand do the same and he was a rustler.

I'd never blotted any brands. I'd never used a cinch ring or a coiled wire or anything to rewrite a brand. Here and there I'd slapped my brand on mavericks I'd come across on the plains. By now there must be several thousand head of stock running loose on the plains that I'd branded.

Suddenly I'd had enough of Brown's Hole. I was going to get out and get out fast.

And that was when I realized somebody was coming down my back trail, somebody hunting me.

7

When I was a small boy I often went to the woods to lie on the grass in the shade. Somehow I had come to believe the earth could give me wisdom, but it did not. Yet I learned a little about animals and learned it is not always brave to make a stand. It is often foolish. There is a time for courage and a time for flight.

There is no man more dangerous than one who does not doubt his own rightness. Long ago I heard a man in the country store near my home say that a just man always had doubts. Dutch Brannenburg had no doubts. And he had gathered about him men who had no doubts. They were not outlaws, they were just hard, cold men who rode for the brand and believed every nester or drifting cowhand if not a thief was at least a potential thief.

They had decided, when they lost the trail of the men they followed, that I must have aided them, and so intended to hang me in their place.

Had I remained on the trail they would have had me now, and as it was they were coming.

Nine hard men with a noose ready for hanging, and me alone with womenfolks over the mountain who waited for my coming.

A draw opened through brush head-high to a horseman, and I turned into it, praying to God that it was not a dead end. My horse was a fast walker, and I walked him now, saving what he had for a time of need.

No more than a quarter of a mile behind, they were working out my trail, and they'd do it, too. I hadn't an idea they would not. I was a good man at hiding a trail, but these were man hunters, cow trackers, Injun fighters. Every man-jack of them was good at reading sign.

Suddenly the canyon branched; I went up the smaller canyon, followed it a couple of hundred yards, and then went to the bank and off through the cedars.

The ridge lay a half mile beyond, and I took off for it, angling up and using all the cover I could find, holding myself on a low angle to keep from their eyes as long as possible. My horse was in fine shape, and it would need to be, for I'm a big man and the trail would be long.

This was no time to lead trouble to Em Talon, so I headed off into broken country. A man who has been riding the wild trails as long as me gets a feel for them and for mountain country. Beyond that ridge up ahead were other ridges, canyons, buttes—a maze of rough country. The last fifty yards lay ahead of me and I glanced back. They were topping out at the canyon's edge, and a far-off shout told me I'd been seen.

They done a foolish thing. They started to run at me.

Being too anxious sometimes can deal a man a hard blow. They rode fast up that slope and there's not much that can take more out of a horse than that. I'd purposely walked my horse, taking it easy. I kept on walking, wanting both to save my mount and give them the idea I did not realize I was being pursued.

Then I topped out on the ridge and went over, onto a long shelf of above-timber line rock. I followed it for fifty yards, then doubled back and rode back on the far side of a V where the ridge had been the point. As they came up one side of the V, I was riding along the other side just over the ridge from them.

Then I trotted my horse. I taken our time, but I pushed just enough to get out of sight in the spruce trees before they topped the ridge. Once in the spruce trees I followed along as I was going, weaving among the trees for a quarter of a mile or so, turning downhill a few yards, then up, riding between trees so close together I had to pull one leg out of a stirrup to get through, crossing bare rock and changing direction as I crossed, or doubling back.

If those boys fitted my neck into their noose they were going to have some riding to do first.

The roan I was riding had been showing me something more than I'd expected. Talon was a horse breeder as well as a builder, and if this horse was any example he was a man with talent. Judging by what Em had said during one of our sort of rambling talks, Talon had bred Morgan stallions to the best of the mustang mares he could find, and the roan seemed to have the brains of the Morgan and the all-around wild animal savvy of the mustang. Since Talon died, most of his stock had been running wild in the mountains, and this roan took to high country like it had known nothing else.

What was important now was that that horse would go just about anywhere I asked it to, and it had been teaching me that most of the horses I'd known up to now were something not to be considered in the same rank with this one.

Riding up through a bunch of cedars, I turned in my saddle and glanced back. They were maybe a thousand feet lower down, and by the way they'd have to ride, a half mile behind. Suddenly I saw a huge boulder—it must've weighed half a ton—balanced beside the game trail I'd come out on as I topped the ridge.

The boulder had tumbled down from a shoulder of higher rock and was held in place by a couple of rocks no bigger than my fist. It had probably been there no longer than since the last windstorm and maybe less. If it started to roll it was going to roll right down on them as they came out of the woods.

Stepping down from the saddle I taken a long pole, the broken trunk of a young spruce, and I jammed the end of it against one of those small rocks. It came loose and

60

the boulder teetered. I smacked it again and that boulder crunched down on what lay ahead and beneath it.

It turned over slowly, majestically, then rolled over again, a bit faster. Right below it was a drop of about six feet and then the steep hillside. It rolled over that drop, hit hard, and then started down the slope followed by an army of smaller stuff, rocks from the size of a man's head to fist-size.

Down below Brannenburg and his men, bunched pretty well, came out of the woods. For a moment there I didn't think they'd see it, then Dutch looked up. As he looked that huge boulder hit a jump off place and must have bounded thirty feet out into the air.

Dutch cut loose with a yell that I heard faintly, and then the bunch scattered . . . only just in time.

One horse hit on a side slope and went rolling, rider and all, another went to pitching as the boulder lit with the shower of rocks coming with it, then rolled off down the slope to lodge in the trees.

I hadn't wanted to kill nobody. I just wanted to slow them up, make them cautious, but they were some shook up, I could see that.

One man had been bucked off and he was getting up, limping. A horse was running away, stirrups slopping. The others were fighting their horses, trying to get them calmed down, and they were having troubles. I just rode off around the knoll and cantered across a long green meadow toward the lip of a basin.

Before reaching it I rode across a great shelving ledge of tilted rock, knowing my horse might leave some hoof scars, but they would be few and the trackers would have to ride slow to read the sign.

There was a steep, winding trail down from the shelf into a basin that lay partly below timberline. A scattering of spruce and foxtail pine had crept up the south-facing slope, and I let the roan pick its way down through the trees.

High on a slope opposite I saw a half dozen bighorn sheep watching me. Their eyes are sharp, and they miss mighty little. A camp-robber jay picked up my trail and followed me along, hoping for some food I might drop, but he was backing the wrong card. I'd no time to stop and dig something out of my outfit.

There are folks who can't abide camp-robber jays, but I take to them. Often enough they've been my only company for days at a time, and they surely do get friendly. They'll steal your grub right from under your nose, but who am I to criticize the life style of a bird? He has his ways, I have mine. Like I say, I take to them.

This was my kind of country. I'm a high-line man. I like the country up yonder where the trees are flagged by the wind, where there's sedge and wild flowers under foot and where the mountains gnaw the sky with gray hard teeth, flecked with a foam of snow gathered in their hollows.

All the time I was working my way east, trying to wear them out or lose them, but drawing closer and closer to the MT ranch and Em Talon.

That night I made no fire. I chewed on some jerky and some rose hips I'd picked from time to time, finished the last small chunk of bread I'd brought, and ate a half dozen wild onions.

Once I'd stripped the gear from the roan I scouted the country around, rifle in hand. There was no way a body could see my camp until they were right up close, and no way anybody could approach without making some noise. I was backed up against the edge of a grove of aspen and I'd picked about the only level spot on a steep hillside.

Before daybreak I was off and riding, heading right off down the valley and paying no mind to my trail. It was rolling up clouds for a heavy rain and whatever tracks I made would soon be gone.

My grub was gone and I was dearly wanting a cup of

coffee when I sighted a ranch house trailing smoke into the rain. First off I pulled up near some trees and gave study to the place. I was a half mile off and five hundred feet higher, and the place lay in a meadow with a trail running past the gate and aspen spilling down the mountainside opposite. Circling around, I came up through the aspen and sat there five minutes or so, studying the house. Finally I decided whoever was there it certainly wasn't the posse. So I rode on in.

I walked my horse up to the house and gave a call and after a bit a door opened. The man in the door had a gun on, and he yelled, "Put up your horse and come in."

I took my horse to the stables and stepped inside. There were four horses there, three of them dry, one wet. I took the roan to a stall and rubbed him down with a handful of hay, then forked some hay into the manger for him. Prying around with a lighted lantern, I found a sack of oats and put a good bait of that in the bin for my horse.

Studying on the situation, I commenced to feel uneasy, but my roan surely needed the grub, and so did I. Slipping the thong from my pistol butt, I went inside the house. The door opened as I walked up.

There was a red-haired girl there, of maybe seventeen years. She had a sprinkling of freckles over her nose and I grinned at her. She looked shy, but she smiled back.

There were three men in the place, all of them armed. One of them, a tall, thin galoot, stooped in the shoulders, had wet boots and the knees of his pants above the boots were wet. He'd been riding in the rain under a slicker.

"Travelin'," I said. "I ran short of grub."

"Set up to the table. There's beef and there's coffee."

The other men bobbed their heads at me, the man with the wet boots slowest of all.

Now excepting that red-headed girl there was nothing about this here setup that I liked. Of course, any man

63

might have been riding this day, but it was uncommon for men to be wearin' guns in the house with a woman— I mean, unless they were fixing to go out again.

The man who seemed to own the place was a stocky gent with rusty hair, darker than the girl's, but they favored and were likely some kin. There was that tall galoot with the wet boots whom the others called Jerk-Line.

"I'm Will Scanlan," the rusty-haired one said. "This here's Jerk-Line Miller and that gent over yonder with the seegar is Benton Hayes."

Scanlan nor Miller I'd not heard tell of. Benton Hayes a man in my line of business would know. He was a scalp-hunter . . . a bounty hunter, if you will. He had a reputation for being good with a gun and not being very particular on how he used it.

"And the lady?" I asked.

"Her?" Scanlan seemed surprised. "Oh, that there's Zelda. She's my sister."

"Favors you," I said. And then added, "My name's Logan. I ride for an outfit over east of here."

The coffee tasted almighty good, but already I was thinking of an excuse for getting out. No traveler in his right mind is going to pick up and leave a warm, dry place for the out-of-doors on a rainy night, and if I did that they'd been bound to get suspicious.

Meanwhile I was putting that beef where it would do the most good. Zelda brought me a healthy chunk of corn pone and a glass of milk to go with it.

"Lots of outfits east of here," Hayes commented. "Any pa'tic'lar one?"

I decided I did not like Mr. Hayes. "The Empty," I said. "I ride for Em Talon."

"Talon?" Benton Hayes frowned. "I've heard that name. Oh, yes! Milo Talon. He's on the list."

"List?" I acted mighty innocent.

"He's a wanted man," Hayes replied.

"Milo? He'd never break no law."

64

"He's on my list, anyways. Somebody wants him and wants him dead."

"Well," I said, smiling friendly-like, "don't try to collect it. Seems to me Milo Talon was kind of quick on the shoot."

"Makes no dif'rence," Hayes said. "They can be had. All of them."

"I'm sure he's not the kind to break the law," I said, still smiling. "Milo was a nice boy. Could it be somebody else wants him?"

"How do I know? He's wanted, somewhere. There's five hundred dollars on him." He shuffled through some notes from an inside pocket. "There it is . . . Jake Flanner, mayor of Siwash. He'll pay it for him or his brother, Barnabas."

"What do you know about that?" I said. Then I yawned. "I'll bunk in the barn," I said, "no use to bother you gents."

"You can sleep here." Scanlan had shot a quick look at the others before he made that offer, and he seemed a mite anxious.

"Zelda, fix Mister Logan a bed in the other room, there." He glanced at me. "You can get to sleep without us botherin' you with our talk."

I taken up my rifle and followed the young lady into the next room where there was a better than usual bed. There was no window in the room, only the door I come through.

Zelda put the light down on a table, then looked at me quickly and whispered, "You watch it, mister. I don't like that Mister Hayes. I don't trust him."

"Neither do I." I grinned at her. "But I do like you, and if I get things straightened around a mite I may just come around this way again."

She looked at me seriously. "Mister," she said quietly, "I favor a man who is willin' to settle down. I don't want to marry up with no man who rides trails by night."

65

"You're a hundred percent right," I said. "Can you make bearsign?"

"Doughnuts? Of course, I can."

"Make some," I said, "and keep them handy. When I come courtin' I'll expect a plate full of doughnuts."

She went out and I taken a quick look around. The man who built this cabin built it to last. He also put in a trapdoor leading to an attic.

8

I put a knee on the bed so's it would creak some, and then I dropped a book on the floor, hoping it would sound like a boot. After a moment, I dropped it again.

Taking the chair I tiptoed over to that trapdoor, put the chair down, and got up on it. Very carefully I put both palms under the door and lifted the least bit. Dust sifted down, and the door moved. Hadn't been opened in a long time. More than likely they no longer thought of it being there.

Easing it aside I grasped the timber with one hand, laid my rifle up with the other, then chinned myself on the edge, hoisting myself up until I could wiggle over onto the floor.

The attic was dark and still and smelled of dust. There was a faint square of light across the room that looked to be a window. Very carefully, I eased myself that way. Near to the chimney I was stopped by a voice.

"He's riding an MT horse, all right. And that's the Talon brand."

66

"I'm tellin' you," Jerk-Line was sayin', "That's got to be him Brannenburg is huntin'. I talked to that posse when they came to the Hoy place, an' they were sore as hell. This here gent had really run their legs off, an' then they lost him."

"Will Brannenburg pay? I hear he's a tough man to deal with." Hayes was talking now.

"We'd better ride over an' see," Scanlan said. "You surely ain't goin' to bluff him into payin' for something he never asked to pay for."

"Jerk-Line," Hayes said. "You ride over. He's at the McNary place tonight. Find out what he'll give for this man's hide. You get him to offer a good sum and we'll split fifty for me, twenty-five each for you."

"Why not in thirds?" Jerk-Line wanted to know.

Benton Hayes's voice was cool. "Because I'm goin' to kill him. All you boys got to do is wait an' watch."

Well, I nearly went back down that trapdoor to give him his chance, but there was three now, and if Dutch did what he'd be likely to do he'd let this man take off on his return trip, then he'd follow. Dutch liked to do his own killing . . . or see it done.

After some more talk Jerk-Line went to the door and went out. I heard him slosh through the mud to the barn, and a moment later I heard his horse pounding off down the road.

I didn't know how far he'd have to go to this McNary place, but I didn't figure to wait. I tried to slip that window at the end of the loft up or down or sideways, but she was fixed in place. Taking out my Tinker-made knife I put the point into the frame and cut deep. That there knife was sharper than a razor. It cut deep, a sliver several inches long, then another. In maybe two shakes of a dog's tail I had cut that window loose from its frame.

Easing myself out I dropped to the ground and stood flat against the wall for a minute. Then I crossed to the barn and saddled my roan. Leading her out I put her in the edge of those aspen, and then I stopped.

That Benton Hayes back there. He was bound and determined to kill me if there was money in it. Well, I wasn't near so greedy.

I walked back to the house and up to the back door. Easing it open, I saw Zelda staring at me wide-eyed. "Get your brother out here," I said.

She hesitated only a moment, then went to the door and said, "Will? Can I talk to you for a minute?"

Scanlan came to the door and stepped in, closing it behind him. "Zel? Can't you see I'm busy? Couldn't this wait?"

"Not if you want to live," I whispered.

He looked at me and that pistol in my hand, and he swallowed. "Mister Scanlan," I said softly, "you got you a fine sister here, but you're trailin' your spurs in mighty poor company. You give me that gun you got, and then you set down yonder, and don't neither of you make a move until I'm gone . . . you hear?"

He nodded, handed me his gun, and edged to the chair. I shoved his gun behind my belt and dropped mine into my holster.

"He figures to hang my hide," I said. "I'm going to see can he do it."

I opened the door and stepped through. Benton Hayes looked up. His expression was kinda sour as he spied me standing there in the doorway.

"Mister Hayes," I said, "you was talkin' a minute ago about selling my hide for a few dollars. You said you would do the killin'. Well, you got you a gun there, let's see you do it."

He got up slowly. He was surprised and scared at first, then the scare left him. "Why, sure. One way is as easy as another, Logan."

"Sackett's the name," I said, "Logan Sackett."

I might as well have kicked him in the belly. His face

68

went taut with a kind of shock, then sick. He was a sure-thing killer who figured he was better than most he'd meet, but I could see he didn't think he was better than Logan Sackett.

Trouble was, he'd already started to draw.

Well, he'd started. So I shucked my old hog-leg and let 'er bang. He taken two of them through the middle button on his vest and just for luck I put another through his Bull Durham tag, where it hung from his left vest pocket.

Then I taken Scanlan's gun from my belt and throwed it free of shells. I left it there on the table when I went down the steps.

The roan was waiting and I swung into the saddle and taken out. I mean, I left there. If Dutch was going to come hunting he'd have to find his game elsewhere. My old pa was never one to let his enemy choose the ground for a difficulty. "Boy," he used to say, "don't you never side-step no fight, not permanent, that is. Just you pick the time and the place."

I taken out and rode over the mountains to where the Empty lay, and I came on her in the fresh light of morning after a night in the saddle. The roan was ga'nted and tired, but he was ready to keep going, knowing the home place was yonder.

We rode in by the back way again, and I stepped down and leaned against the door there for a minute, dead beat.

That girl, she came out the door, looking perky as all get-out, but scared too when she seen me leaning.

"*Oh!* Logan, are you hurt?" She ran to me, and caught me by the hand to look at me the better, and I was ashamed to see her stare at me so with old Em looking down from the doorway.

"I ain't hurt." Maybe my voice was a mite rough. "I've come a fur piece."

"There's coffee on," Em said, her being the practical one, "come in an' set."

When I'd stripped the gear from the roan and cared for it, I went into the house. First off, I walked through and looked out front.

Nothing.

And that scared me. Jake Flanner wasn't a forgetting man.

We set about the table and I told them about my ride, my meeting with Brannenburg, and that Flanner had put a price on her sons' heads.

She was furious. Her old eyes turned hard and she asked, "Where'd you hear *that?*"

"A man named Benton Hayes . . . a bounty hunter."

"Is he hunting my boys? Is he?"

"No ma'am, he ain't huntin' nobody. He give it up."

She looked me through. "Ah? You read him from the Book, then?"

"Well, ma'am, he had him a sheaf of papers, names of men to be hunted and the money to be paid for them, and I heard him tell those other men that Brannenburg wanted me enough to pay money for it.

"You see, ma'am, he might have come huntin' me, layin' for me like, when I was breakin' a horse or mendin' fence or somewhat. I decided if he wanted my hair he should have his chance without wastin' no more time."

"And?"

"He wasn't up to it, ma'am. He just wasn't up to it." I emptied my cup and reached for the pot. "Seems like in a new country like this, ma'am, so many men choose the wrong profession. You can't tell. In something else he might have made good."

Three days went by like they'd never been. I was busy workin' around the place from can-see to cain't-see. I even ploughed a vegetable garden with some half-broke broncs who'd no notion of ploughin' anything. I harrowed

70

that same ground and planted Indian corn, pumpkins, onions, radishes, melons, beans, peas, and what-not. And I surely ain't no farmer.

Why, I hadn't done the like since I left that side-hill farm in the Clinch Mountains. Up there in those Tennessee hills we had land so rocky the plants had to push rocks away to find room to grow in. We used to have to put pegs alongside our melons to keep 'em from rolling down into the next farm. I heard tell of a Tennessee farm where there was two brothers each having a short leg. One had a left leg short, the other a right leg, but they worked out the ploughin' just fine. One would take the plough goin' out where his long leg would be downhill, then his brother'd be waitin' for him to plough back the same way.

On the third night we sat about the table, Em Talon, Pennywell, an' me, rememberin' the pie suppers, barn-raisin's, and such-like back to home. We were poor folks in the hills, but we had us a right good time. Somebody always brung along a jug or two of mountain lightning, and toward morning there'd be some real old hoedown and stick-your-thumb-in-their-eyes fightin'. A time or two it would get serious and the boys would have at each other with blades.

Mostly it was just good old-fashioned fun and yarnin' around the pump out back of the house between dances.

All we needed was a mountain fiddler. Come to think of it we didn't even need him. Sometimes we'd just sing our own tunes to dance by, such as "Hello, Susan Brown!" or "Green Coffee Grows on High Oak Trees."

With moonrise I taken my Winchester and went outside to feel of the wind. Wandering off toward the gate I listened. For a long time there I heard nothing but the wind in the grass and then I thought I heard something, so I lay down and put an ear to the ground.

Riders coming up the trail, several of them. I checked

the lock on the gate, then faded back into the darkness toward the house.

They came on, quite a bunch of them. They stopped by the gate and there was sort of an argument there.

Suddenly a board in the floor creaked and I turned my head. Em Talon was standing there with her Sharps Fifty and she said, "Logan, you better go inside. Those men aren't Flanner's outfit."

"How do you know that?"

She ignored that, but simply said, "I think it's Dutch Brannenburg, huntin' you."

We heard a faint rattle from the gate, which was locked, and Em up with her Sharps and put a bullet toward the gate. Somebody swore and we heard them moving off a bit.

"You go to sleep, Logan," Em said. "I'm an old woman and it don't take much. You've had a hard time of it these past days."

"This here is my trouble," I protested.

"No, it ain't. You're ridin' for me, now. I knew Dutch when he first came into this country, singin' mighty small. He hadn't any of those biggety notions he's got now. A man's only king as long as folks let him be. You leave him to me."

Em Talon was not a woman you argued with, so I turned around, went inside, and bedded down. Besides, I had a good notion they'd wait until morning. Hanging a drifter was one thing, attacking a ranch with the reputation the MT had was another.

For the first time in a long while I slept sound the night through and only awoke when the sunlight filtered through the shutters. Opening my eyes, I listened but heard nothing. Then I got out of bed, put on my hat, and got dressed. What I saw in the mirror looked pretty sorry, so I stropped my razor on a leather belt, then shaved.

Somebody tapped on the door. It was Pennywell. "You'd better come," she said, "there's trouble."

Picking up my gun belt I slung it around my hips and cinched up, then I slipped the thong from my pistol and went into the hall.

"What's happening?"

Pennywell pointed and held up a finger for silence.

The door was open and Emily Talon was on the porch. There were a bunch of riders settin' their horses at the door, and I heard Em's voice.

"Dutch Brannenburg, what do you mean ridin' in here like this? You never were very bright, but just what do you think you're doing? Riding in here, hunting one of my men?"

"I want that Logan, Missus Talon, an' I want him now."

"What do you want him for?"

"He's a damn' thief, Missus Talon. He deserves hangin'."

"What did he steal? Any of your horses?"

Brannenburg hesitated. "He was one of them stole my horses. We trailed two thieves an' we come on him, he—"

"When were your horses stolen?"

"About ten days back, an'—"

"Logan has been working for me for several weeks, and he hasn't been off the place until he rode over to Brown's Hole."

"He killed a man," Dutch protested. "He shot a man over west of here."

"You damned right he did." Em Talon's voice was cold. "I know all about Benton Hayes, a dry-gulching, back-shootin' murderer who has had it coming for years. If he hadn't shot him, I might have.

"Now, Dutch, you turn your horses around and you ride out of here. You ever bother an Empty hand again and I'll nail your hide to the fence.

"I recall when you first come into this country, Dutch,

73

and I recall when you branded your first stock. You've become high an' mighty here these past few years, but if you want to rake up the past, Dutch, I can tell some stories."

Brannenburg's face flushed. "Now, see here, Missus Talon, I—"

"You ride out of here, Dutch, or I'll shoot you my ownself."

Dutch was angry. He did not like being faced down by a woman, but he remembered this one, and she could be a holy terror when she got started.

"I want Logan," Dutch insisted. "That man's a thief. Why else did he run when chased?"

"You'd run from a lynch party, too, Dutch." She looked down at him from the porch, and then suddenly she said, "Dutch, do you really want him? Do you just have to have Logan?"

Suddenly wary, Dutch peered at her, trying to read what was in her mind.

"That's what we come for," he said sullenly. "We come after him."

"I've heard all about your lynching cow thieves, or them you thought were thieves, and I heard you set fire to a couple of them. All right, Dutch, you want Logan, I'll give him to you."

"What?" Dutch peered at her. "What's that mean?"

"Logan Sackett," she said quietly, "is kin of mine. We come of the same blood. I'm a Sackett, same as him, and I know my kinfolk. Now you boys believe in fair play, don't you?" she spoke to Brannenburg's riders.

"Yes, ma'am, we surely do. Yes, ma'am."

"All right, Dutch. You want Logan Sackett. I hear tell you shape yourself around as something of a fighter. You been walking hard-heeled around this country for several years now because most of these folks hadn't lived here long enough to know you when you walked almighty soft. You just get down off your horse, Dutch. You want

74

Logan, you can have him. You can have him fist and skull right here in front of my stoop, and the first one of your boys who tries to help you will get a bullet through his brisket."

Well, I just walked out on the porch and stopped on the steps. "How about it, Dutch? You want to take me, it's like Em says. You got to do it yourself, with your own hands an' without help."

9

Well, his face was a study, believe me. He was mad clean through but there just wasn't anything he could do but fight. Dutch sat up there on his horse and he knew he had it to do. Em Talon had laid it out for him and there was no way out short of looking small before his men, and no ranch boss of a tough outfit dares do that.

He got down off his horse and trailed his reins. He taken off his gun belt and slung it around the horn, and then he hung his hat over it.

Meanwhile I'd unslung my gun and knife and come down off the porrch. When he turned around I knew I was in for trouble. I was taller than him, but he was broad and thick and would outweigh me by fifteen pounds or so. He was shorter, but he was powerful and he moved in, hands working back and forth.

I moved out toward him, a little too confident maybe. He taken that out of me but quick. Suddenly he charged, and he was close in before he did, and he went low into a crouch, swinging both hands high. One of them crossed my left shoulder and connected like a thrown brick.

Right away I knew that whatever else Dutch was, he was a scrapper. Somewhere along the line of years behind him he'd learned how to fight. He came up inside, butting his head, then back-heeling me so I fell to the ground. I rolled over and he put the toe of a boot into my ribs before I could get up and raked me with his spur as his foot swung back from the kick. He raked back and he raked deep, ripping my shirt and leaving a trail of blood across my chest. I was up then, but he came at me, and I knew this wasn't just a fight. He was out to kill me.

You think it can't be done? I've seen a half dozen men killed in fights, and there was no mercy in Dutch, nor in any of his boys. Nor in Em Talon, for that matter.

He came at me, boring in, punching, driving, stomping on my insteps when he got close, raking my shins with the sides of his boots or his spurs. And it taken me a moment to get started.

He was a bull. He had great powerful shoulders under that shirt, and he slammed in close, butting me under the chin with his head. I threw him off and he charged right back. I managed to slam a right into his ribs as he came close, but he knew where he had to win that fight, and that was in close where I couldn't use my longer arms.

He slammed away at my belly, and I taken a few wicked punches. Then I slammed him on the side of the face with an elbow smash that cut to the bone. When that blood started to show, Dutch went berserk. It was like roping a cyclone. He slammed at me and every punch hurt. He was fighting to kill, but I shoved him off, stiffened a fist into his face, then caught him with a right as he came on in.

It stopped his rush, shook him to his heels. I landed a left and then, as he crouched, swung a right to that split cheekbone that ripped the cut wider.

He hit me twice in the ribs, charged on in, head under

my chin, and I tripped and went down. He came down on top of me, grabbing for my throat. I reached across one of his arms, grabbed the other, and jerked. He rolled over and I got to my feet first. I started for him as he started to roll and he lashed out at me with both spurred heels. I jumped back just in time to get a wicked slash across one wrist. Then he came up and I hit him in the mouth.

It smashed his lips back into his teeth. He came at me again and I split his ear with a left hook, turning him half around. He grabbed my arm and tried to throw me with a flying mare but I went with it and put both knees into his back. He went down hard, me on top. Grinding his face into the dust, I had him half smothered before I suddenly let go and jumped back. I wanted to whip him, not kill him.

He came up from the ground, staggered, located me and rushed. I put a left jab to his mouth, and as he came close caught him under the chin with the butt of my palm and slammed his head back.

There was no quit in him, I'll give him that. He was bull-strong and iron-hard and his punching away at my belly was doing me no good. I shoved him off, hit him with a stunning right as he tried to come in again, and then I let him come, but turned a little as he came in and threw him over his hip with a rolling hip lock. He came down hard in the dust.

"Dutch," I said, "you know damn well I never stole any stock of yours. An' you know I didn't know those two who did."

Paying me no mind, he got up on his hands and knees, then threw himself in a long dive at my legs. My knee smashed him in the face as he came in, and he fell, but he rolled over and came up again.

"You fight pretty good, Dutch," I said, "but it takes more than owning a lot of cows to make a big man. Hanging anybody you can find or anybody you don't like makes you nothing but a murderer, lower than any of the men you chase."

He wiped the blood from his face with his sleeve and stared at me. His cheek was cut to the bone, his lips were in shreds. One eye had a gray lump over it, but he stood there, his big hands opening and closing, the hatred in his eyes an ugly thing.

"You want some more, Dutch," I said, "you come an' get it."

"Next time," he said, "it'll be with a gun."

He wasn't stopped. I'd beaten him, but he wasn't through. He liked too much what he thought he'd become. He liked the feeling of power, liked walking hard-heeled down the boardwalks of the towns, liked being followed by a lot of tough riders, with people stepping out of the way.

Most of them were just being polite in spite of his rudeness, but he thought they were afraid. He liked bullying people, liked shoving them around. And he wasn't going to give it up because he'd lost a fist fight.

One of his riders spoke up. "When he comes, Sackett, he won't be alone. We'll all come with him. And we'll bring a rope."

"You do that," I said, "he'll need all the help he can get."

They turned their horses and rode away. At the gate one of them got down and opened the gate, then fastened it again. That was cattle country . . . nobody left a gate down when it was there to close.

"Thanks, Em," I said. "That could have been rough."

"It was rough. But it ain't the first time. It used to be Injuns when pa was away."

"Logan?" Pennywell tugged at my sleeve. "Let me fix up your face."

My face was bruised and battered some, although I'd no bad cuts. Dutch had been a lot more of a fighter than I figured him for and he'd battered my ribs something

78

awful. I never said nothing even when Pennywell hurt my face, fixing it up.

Late that night, stretched on my bed, I swore softly. As if Em Talon hadn't enough trouble! I'd brought more upon her in the shape of Brannenburg. He was a vindictive man, and those who rode for him were a rougher crowd then you'd usually find on a cow outfit. Cowhands could be almighty rough, but this bunch were trouble hunters. Many of them had taken a turn at being outlaws, gun hands and whatever the occasion demanded . . . like me.

The trouble was, I'd brought them down on Em Talon.

I never was no hand for figurin'. I've seen folks set down an' ponder on things until they saw their way clear, but me, I was never no hand at that. I'm strong and mean, but I never found no way of doing things except to walk right out and take the bull by the horns. Settin' an' waitin' rankled. I wasn't geared for it. I needed a problem where I could walk out swinging both fists. Nolan was more inclined to study on things. Me, it was always root hog or die, and that was what I needed right now.

Troubles were bunching around us. Everywhere I looked I could see it shaping up like thunderheads gathering over the high peaks. Jake Flanner was cooking up something, and now Dutch would be also.

It was right about then that I decided I'd better go right after them instead of settin', waitin', and finally getting clobbered.

Some folks take to running. Some folks hope that by backing up far enough they'll not have trouble, but it surely doesn't work. I'd ridden all over the Rio Grande, Mogollon, Mimbres, La Plata, and Mesa Verde country and what I saw was a lesson.

The Indians there were good Indians, planting Indians. For a long time they lived in peace and bothered nobody, and then Navajo-Apache tribes came migrating down the east side of the Rockies. They found a way west without climbing over mountains. Those nice, peaceful tribes along the Rio Grande were shoved right off the map. Some were killed, some fled to western lands and built cliff houses, but you couldn't escape by running. The Navajo followed them right along, killing and destroying. Had they banded together under a good leader and waited they might have held the Navajo off, but when danger showed, a family or group of families would slip away to avoid trouble, and those left would be too few to hold off the enemy.

Finally most of them were killed, the cliff houses fell into ruins, the irrigation projects they'd started fell apart. The wild tribes from out of the wilderness had again won a battle over the planting peoples . . . so it had always been.

I'd ridden through that country, I'd seen the broken pottery and the deserted villages. Farther west I'd find more of the pottery and more ruins. Sometimes you'd find where groups of Indians had merged, but it was always the same. They'd pull out rather than make a stand, and they saw all they'd built fall apart, saw their people cut down, saw their world fall apart.

A couple of times hiding out in canyons I'd come on some of those cliff dwellings. I never told nobody about them because I wouldn't have been believed. To most white men all Indians were blanket Indians. Several times I'd holed up in a cliff dwelling, drinking water from their springs, sometimes finding remnants of their corn fields where volunteer corn stalks had grown up after constant reseeding of itself.

I had a warm feeling for those folks, and sometimes of a night I'd lie there where they slept. One night I awakened filled with terror. I got up and looked out the window over the moonlit canyons and I fancied I could hear them coming, hear the wild Navajo coming out of the wilderness to attack the peaceful villages. The terror I felt was the terror they must have felt, even when they moved on they'd know it was only a matter of time.

Sometimes only a few warriors would come filtering through the canyons, killing a farmer at work or shooting his wife off a ladder where she climbed with her child. A few would come, but they'd wait around until more came, and more. Up in the cliff dwellings the people would wait, looking down, seeing their crops reaped by others or destroyed, seeing them gather there, knowing someday they would come in sufficient numbers and the floors of the cliff houses would be dark with blood. Some of the people would climb out over the tops of the cliffs and escape, some would try and be killed in the process.

It was like Em Talon. Her husband had been murdered, her hands killed or driven off. Little by little they had gone until she had stood alone against them, a tall old woman, alone in her bleak mansion, waiting for the day when she could no longer lift the Sharps or see to fire it.

I'd come drifting along, a man with no good reputation behind him. I was one of the savages, one of the wanderers. I was no planting Indian, no planter at all. I was a drifter, a man who lived by the gun. But I'd dug in here and stayed . . . now the time had come to carry it to them.

I'd had enough of waiting. I wasn't going to sit and let them bring death to me and to this old woman. I was going after them. I was going to root them out, throw them out, burn them out, or die trying. It just wasn't in me to set and wait.

Like I said, I'm no hand at figuring. It's my way to just bull in and let the chips fall where they will, but I did give thought to getting into the town unseen, and to getting away when it was over . . . if there was anything of me left.

Not even a mouse will trust himself to only one hole, so I sat back and recalled the town, thinking out where the buildings and the corrals were situated. Somewhere along the line, sleep fetched itself to me.

At breakfast Em was in a talking mood. She had been up shy of daylight, peering out through the shutters, studying out the land.

"You should have seen it when me an' Talon came west," she said. "There was nobody out thisaway, just nobody at all. Talon had been far up the Missouri before this, on a steamboat, and he'd been up the Platte as far as a boat could go. He'd seen his buffalo and killed a grizzly or two, and he'd lived and traveled among Injuns, and fit with them a time or two.

"We come west and he kept a-tellin' me of this place, and me, I was ready for it. I was a mountain gal, raised back yonder in the hills, and all that flat land worried me, nothing moving but the grass before the wind and maybe an antelope far away or a herd of buffalo.

"Then we seen this place. We seen it from afar off, standing out on the grassland with the mountains behind. Talon had left four mountain men in a cabin on the land, but they weren't needed.

"At first the Injuns just came to look, to stare at the three-story house looming above the country around. They called it the wooden tepee and sat their horses in astonishment, gaping at the house that had appeared like a miracle, for the Indians had been gone on the annual buffalo hunt when the house was built.

"When the Cheyennes rode up to see, Talon went out to meet them. He took them, four at a time, through the house, showing them everything, from the enormous stretch of country that could be seen from the railed walk atop the house to the loopholes from which shots could be fired while the shooter was safe within.

"He knew the story would be told, and he wanted them to know they could be seen a long time before they
82

reached the house, and that an attacker could be fired upon from any place within the house."

"But you've so much furniture!" Pennywell exclaimed. "How ever did you get it out here?"

"Talon made some of it. Like I said, he was handy. The rest of it we brought out. Talon had trapped for fur, and he kept on trapping. He found some gold here and yon in the mountain streams, and he ordered what he had a mind to. We brought us a whole wagon train of things out from the east, for Talon liked to live well, and that's the sort of thing you break into mighty easy."

Sittin' back in that big hidebound chair I could see behind her words. Seeing the Indians filtering back from their hunt, riding through an area they probably only saw once or twice a year, anyway, to find this great house reared up, staring out over the plains with the great, empty eyes of its windows.

To them it must have been a kind of magic. It had been built quickly. Talon was a driving man, by all accounts, and the mountain men he had helping him were not the kind to stay in one place for long. How many he had to help Em never said, but there were four who had lived in a cabin on the place while Talon rode east to find his bride. There might have been more.

Probably Talon and Sackett had framed much of the structure before their help arrived, and certainly the plan must have been put together in his mind whilst working on the rivers or building for other men.

Sitting there, eyes half closed, listening to her tell it in that old Tennessee mountain tone of hers, I found myself getting restless again. Nobody had the right to take from them what they had built.

Me, I was never likely to build anything. A no-account drifter like me leaves no more mark behind him then you leave a hole in the water when you pull your finger out. Every man could leave something, or should.

Well, maybe it wasn't in me to build much, but I surely could keep the work of other men from being destroyed.

I was going to ride into Siwash and open the place up. I was going in there and drive Len Spivey and his kind clear out of the country.

I'd go tonight.

10

Now I never laid claim to having no corner on brains, and most of what I picked up in the way of knowledge was knocked into my head one way or the other. What I've learned, or most of it, has been concerned with just staying alive.

Guns, horses, hitches, and half-nelson's are more in line with my thinking, but here and there just plain looking and seeing what you look at has taught me something. Also, whilst never much of a hand to go to the mat with a book, I'm a good listener.

Folks who have lived the cornered sort of life most scholars, teachers, and storekeepers live seldom realize what they've missed in the way of conversation. Some of the best talk and the wisest talk I've ever heard was around campfires, in saloons, bunkhouses, and the like. The idea that all the knowledge of the world is bound up in schools and schoolteachers is a mistaken one.

There have been a lot of men who just didn't give a damn about tending store or keeping school but who just cut loose their moorings and went adrift.

Wandering men see a lot, and all knowledge is a matter of comparison and the deductions made from it. Moreover, in any crowd of drifters you'll find men of the finest scholastic education as well as men who have just seen a lot and have been putting two and two together.

One time or another I've heard a lot of campfire talk about towns and how they came to be, and a good many sprang up from river crossings. Folks like to camp close to streams for the sake of water, but crossing a big river was quite an operation, so they'd go into camp after they'd crossed over. That is, the smart ones would. Those who went into camp to cross over in the morning often found the water so high come morning they were stuck for several days.

Rome, London, Paris . . . all of them sprang from river crossings, and usually there was some bright gent around who was charging toll to cross over. Any time you find a lot of people who have to have something or do something you'll also find somebody there charging them for doing it.

When people stop at a stream crossing they camp and look around, and you can bet somebody has set up store with things for them to want.

The town of Siwash came to be in just that way. The stream was no great shakes, but there was a good flowing spring, and a man came in, stopped his travels, and began raising sheep. A few months later a man came along headed for the Colorado gold fields, he seen that spring and knowing that water was sometimes more precious than gold, waited until the sheepman's back was turned and then split his skull with an ax, buried him deep, and planted a crop of corn and melons over the ground where he buried the sheepman.

It was the age-old conflict between the farmer and the stock raiser that probably began when Cain killed Abel. Cain was not only the first farmer according to the Good Book, but he built the first city mentioned in the Bible, and this farmer, seeing that lots of people stopped at his spring for fresh water, set up store and began selling vegetables and corn.

He would probably have done all right in the fullness of time but for a gambler with rheumatism in his hands. The gambler rode into town and stopped to watch the business. He listened to the rustle of the cottonwood leaves and the lovely sound of flowing water from the spring, and that night he brought out a greasy deck of cards. Rheumatism in the hands was spelling his finish as a gambler, but those hands still were good enough to deal three queens to Cain.

Cain hadn't seen a woman for a long time so when those three queens showed up together he overrated their value, and when the rheumatic gambler showed his four aces Cain discovered he was no longer a farmer and keeper of a store but a wanderer. The gambler wanted him out of there so he made him a present of his horse . . . and perhaps with a warning from a friendly ghost, he didn't turn his back when Cain picked up his ax. So Cain rode out into the world again, and the gambler became a storekeeper and a tiller of the fields.

He called the place Siwash. Nobody knew why, including him. The name came to him, and he used it. By that time he was selling supplies to the MT ranch, and to several others in the vicinity.

Siwash wasn't a big town. A man with good legs could walk all around it in five minutes, but you could have done the same thing with the first settlement of Troy, which also was built around a spring and on a trade route.

The gambler with the rheumatic hands was still there, and his hands were in even worse shape. The hands that could no longer deal one off the bottom or build up a bottom stock couldn't handle a gun either, so the oldest citizen in Siwash was also the most peaceful.

When Jake Flanner showed up and began quietly taking over the gambler considered shooting him until he saw what happened to several others with the same idea. So he smiled at Jake's stories and kept a gun handy just in case.

Nevertheless, he harbored no good wishes for Flanner; he wished the man out of there, and not merely because he wanted to be top dog. The gambler's name was Con Wellington, and his hands being what they were he wanted peace. It took no wise man to see that there would never be peace where Jake Flanner was. So Con Wellington waited, listened, and bided his time, and as all things eventually came to him, he knew Flanner had been stopped cold by Emily Talon and Logan Sackett.

Logan was no stranger. They'd never been friends, had scarcely met, in fact. Logan had once sat in a poker game with Wellington, whose hands were not rheumatic at the time, but Con knew a good deal about Logan Sackett and he dealt his cards with extreme care.

He was considering some way of getting word to Logan without Flanner's spies telling of it when there was a tap on his window.

Con's mind worked swiftly. Jake Flanner or his men would come to the front door, hence if somebody came to the window it had to be an enemy of Flanner's, and an enemy of Flanner's was always welcome . . . so long as Flanner didn't know about it.

He opened the window a bare inch. "Who is it?" He was studying the background as he asked the question. It was unlikely anybody would be hiding and watching the back of his store, which was also his dwelling, but he was not a trusting man.

"Open your door," I said, and heard him mutter something from within. I'd left my horse under the cottonwoods beside the stream and had come on foot to the Wellington store.

There was a moment of movement within, and then after a bit, a door opened into darkness. "Come in then, and make it quick."

Once inside, Con Wellington uncovered a lantern. "I had an idea it would be you," he said. "There's nobody else would come to me in the night."

He sat down on his bed. It was an old four-poster and the springs creaked heavily as Wellington seated himself, leaving the chair for me.

"It's about Flanner you've come," he said abruptly. "Well, understand me. I don't like the man but he's left me alone. Granted, my business is less than half what it was, but I'm alive, and some are not."

He opened a cigar box and took one himself before pushing it over to me. He lifted his hands, gnarled and twisted from rheumatism. "I've as much nerve as the next man, I think, but with these nerve doesn't matter. I can pull a trigger if I've plenty of time . . . I could still hunt buffalo. But to pull a gun against another man? I'd not have a chance."

"It isn't a gun you'll need. It's another thing I have in mind."

Wellington looked at me sharply. "Logan, you've tied in with Em Talon . . . what's in that for you?"

"We're kinfolk. She was a Clinch Mountain Sackett before she married Talon."

"A Clinch Mountain Sackett may mean something to you. It doesn't to me."

"It means little to anybody but us," I told him. "We set store by kinfolk. We've our troubles, time to time, but when one of us is in danger, there'll be help from any who are around."

Wellington lit his cigar. "I wish my folks were like that. They were glad to be rid of me. My family had money, education, pride of family. So when I lost my money and got into difficulties they threw me out."

"It happens." I lit my cigar, too. It was a good one. "I had a hunch," I said, "that you didn't care for Flanner. Now I want you to stand aside."

"No more?"

"I'm gettin' tired of him. So's Em. Her son's comin' home but he may take a time gettin' here and I want action. I'm goin' to run him out."

"You? And who else?"

"I don't need nobody else. I figured you would know who his friends were. I don't aim to hurt innocent bystanders if it can be helped."

He looked at me, long and thoughtful, and then he said, "You know, I think you might do it." He looked at the long ash on his cigar, then very carefully knocked it off on the edge of his saucer. "Most of the people here don't like him, but right now there's not more than twenty to twenty-five people in town aside from Flanner and his men."

He named them for me, told me where they were likely to be, described a few of them. "The hotel, saloon, and livery stable, and the bunkhouse back of the stable, that's where most of his boys will be. Flanner sticks close to the hotel."

"How about that other one?"

"Johannes Duckett?" Wellington squinted his eyes. "He might be anywhere. He might be outside this minute. He moves around like a ghost."

He paused a moment. "Don't belittle the folks here in town. Jake swings a wide loop but he's left them strictly alone. He shows up at the dances, pie suppers, and the like, and he contributes to get the minister to come to town. They don't like him much, but they've little to complain about.

"They figure his business with the MT is his business. Not many folks around here knew the Talons. They kept to themselves pretty much, and then after the old man was killed Em came to town mighty seldom . . . and after a while, not at all.

"Some of them are jealous. After all, the Talon outfit is big. Most of these folks were latecomers, and none of them realize what it takes to put a big outfit together, especially when the Talons came here."

"They'll stay out of it then?"

89

"I expect so. Naturally, I can promise nothing except for myself."

What my next step would be I simply did not know. Like I said, I'm not long on planning. I just start moving and let things happen. The only planning I do, you might say, is to see that I don't hurt any innocent bystanders. And that was why I risked my neck to come in and talk to Con Wellington.

Suddenly I had a hunch. I wasn't going back the way I came in. If this here Johannes Duckett was laying for me it would be out back, so I'd go right out the front door.

Wellington didn't like it much, but he agreed Duckett might be lying in wait out yonder in the dark, so I went to the front door of the store.

"If they see me and ask about it, tell them I'm running scared but wanted tobacco. I'm not that much of a smoker, but they don't know that. I've seen men risk their necks for a smoke."

Wellington took down a couple of sacks of tobacco. "Just in case," he said.

The door was well oiled, and I slipped out to the boardwalk without a sound. Four long strides and I was across the street, ducking into the space between two buildings. Carefully I worked my way back to my horse.

When I was crouched down near some stumps, looking through the brush at my horse, I saw a man come out of the trees near the road. He looked left and right, then came on. He saw the horse and I heard him give a muttered exclamation, then he reached over and pulled the slip knot I'd tied in the bridle reins. He gathered the reins and was just throwing a leg over the saddle when I heard a shot.

The roan jumped and the strange rider toppled from its back into the grass. The roan ran out of there, head high, reins trailing.

From behind me and to my left there was movement.

I waited, and then a tall, thin man came out of the trees and walked down to the dead man. He struck a match, then swore.

"Wrong man again, Duckett?" I yelled into the darkness.

He turned and shot. It was one move, only I had already fired. He had shot at sound and he missed by a hair. My bullet smacked hard against something metallic, then ricochetted off into the night.

Moving swiftly, I went through the trees, angling toward the road to try to head off my horse.

There were no more shots, no sound. The moon was just showing on the trail and there was a smell of dust in the air. I walked along holding to the shadowed side of the trail, and sure enough, about of a quarter of a mile up the road I found the roan. The horse came to me when I spoke, and I petted it and talked to it for a while before stepping into the saddle.

It was near daybreak when I got back to the ranch.

11

Pennywell was on the lookout when I came in, and when I got inside she brought me a cup of coffee. "Em's asleep," she said, "catching up on some of that lost time."

She studied me critically. I looked beat. After I'd caught my horse I'd had to hightail it for the MT, careful to leave no sign they could use, so I'd come right down the trail and through the main gate.

"Looks like you been out among 'em," she commented. "I frown on that as Em would say."

Explaining what happened, I added, "The way I figure it, Duckett spotted me when I came in and laid for me near my horse. Meanwhile some other of Flanner's men saw me in town, saw me go into or come out of the store, and got ahead of me, planning to get my horse and then me."

"But you shot Duckett?"

"Shot at him. From the sound I must have hit his rifle or a tree near him. I doubt if I did him any harm, but he came within an inch or less of nailing me. That man can shoot, an' Lordy, is he quick!"

"Teach you to go gallivanting around in the middle of the night. Wait for them to come to you."

"I'm a poor hand at waitin'. My style is to carry it to them, show them a fight has two sides."

"Do you think this will do it?"

"Well," I commented, "I've an idea they'll think twice before they open a door. They know I'm huntin' them, too, and that can be a worrisome thing."

Two slow days went by while I worked around the place. One day I rode to the hills and shot an elk, bringing the meat down to the place. I also taken my iron out to the meadows, roped and branded a couple of yearlings.

No work had been done around there for some time and it would be a rustler's dream to get back in there and find all that fine stock wearing no brands. After that I decided to carry an iron with me wherever I went on MT range.

Johannes Duckett didn't shape up like the kind of man who would sit by and let me get away with shooting at him. I knew I'd be hearing from him, with or without Flanner, and I also figured Duckett would go a-prowling for me. He was the kind who would be apt to shoot from anywhere, so I kept off the skyline, rode through the edge of the trees, kept myself out of range as well as I could when I'd no idea where the attack would come from or when.

Nonetheless I still had an idea of riding into Siwash and making myself known.

Em was on the lookout when she seen a rider coming. She turned to me. "Logan? What do you make of him?"

He was coming down the road at a walk, heading for the main gate. Through the glasses I could see he was riding a beat-up buckskin. He was a small-sized man with a narrow-brimmed hat, a speckled shirt and vest. Light glinted from his eyes so I reckoned him for glasses. He was wearing a six-shooter and he had him a rifle shoved down into a boot.

As he rode up to the gate he suddenly touched a spur to his buckskin and I'll be damned if that horse didn't just sail right over a six-bar gate that was all of five feet tall, and did it with no particular mind, sort of offhand and easy.

Em, she taken up her Sharps and that ol' gun boomed as she put a bullet right into the dust ahead of him.

The rider he just taken off his hat, held it high, and waved it down in a low bow. But he kept comin'.

I hitched my Colt into a better position and walked out front. Nobody else was in sight, and I figured to be all ready for this man, whoever he was.

He came on up, walking his horse, and about fifty feet off he drew rein and looked at the house. For a long time he looked, then he dropped his eyes to me. One eye was covered with a kind of white film . . . I reckon he could only see from one.

"You'll be Logan Sackett, I expect? I've come here to join you."

"What for?"

The man did not smile. "The word is that you are about to be run off. Flanner is recruiting fighters. I am Albani Fulbric, and my people have been fighting on the

93

wrong side for a thousand years. I see no reason to change now."

"Can you fight?"

"With any weapon . . . any one at all."

"Well, it's gettin' on to supper time. Come in an' set and we'll talk it over."

He was an odd man with an odd name, but somehow I liked the cut of him. At table he showed himself a fair hand at putting away grub, although in size he wasn't more than two-thirds of me.

"Where'd you get a name like that?" I asked him.

"Names are how you look at 'em. My name is funny to you, yours is funny to me. Sackett—ever listen to the sound of that? Think on it, my friend."

He reached for the beef. "Now you take my name. My folks, both sides of them, come over from Normandy with William the Conqueror. One of them was squire to Sir Hugh de Malebisse and the other rode with Robert de Brus.

"Neither one of them had anything but strong arms and the willingness to use them. One was an Albani, one a Fulbric, and you will find their names in the Doomsday Book. Bold men they were and we who follow their steps are proud to bring no shame to the names they left us."

"They were knights?" Pennywell asked.

"They were not. They were simple men, smiths and the like, between wars. One of them settled in Yorkshire with Sir Hugh, and the other went off to Scotland, hard by. And one of the family later helped to put a Bruce on the throne of Scotland, although a lot of good it did either of them."

I knew nothing of foreign wars or foreign parts, and the talk when not of horses and cattle or buffalo or guns was scarcely easy for me to follow, but there was a lilt to his voice like he was speaking of magic, and I liked to hear what he was saying. The names meant nothing to me, nothing at all.

94

"I've heard those names," Em Talon said. "Talon spoke of them. His family came from France, and by all accounts a roistering lot they were, building ships and sailing them to foreign parts, and more often than not on voyages of piracy. It's a wonder they weren't hanged."

"Are you a hand with cattle?" I asked him.

"I am that. I'll handle a rope with any man, and my horse is good with cattle. I'll earn my keep and whatever it is you'll pay.

"That horse you see me riding has been hard used, but don't look down upon him. He's carried me into and out of much trouble, and time and again we've been to the wars. Let me put a loop over anything that walks, and that buckskin will hold it, whatever it is.

"In the saddle of that horse I'd not be afraid to rope a Texas cyclone, rope and hog-tie it, too. He'll climb where it would put scare into a mountain goat, and one time when a man holed me with a Winchester slug, he carried me fifteen miles through the snow, then pawed on the stoop until folks came to the door to take me down.

"You can call me a dog if you will, sir, but you speak ill of my horse and I'll put lead into you."

"I'd never speak ill of any man's horse," I said sincerely. "I've ridden his kind, and we've a few fit to run with him right here on the Empty."

If Albani was a fair hand at the table he was a better one in the field. We turned to and roped and branded fourteen head the following morning, cleaned out a waterhole where there'd been a slide, and checked out the grass on the upper meadows. He was a handy man with tools and not backward about using them, but I was wary. He'd not said much about himself beyond running off at the head about those old ancestors of his who came over . . . from where I wasn't sure. I'd never heard of Normandy until Pennywell, who reads a lot of books, told me it was in France and that the Normans were originally called Northmen or Vikings, and they'd settled in there where the country looked good. Well, that made sense. Most of us who came west were wishful of the same thing.

Al—as we came to call him—was as good at working on fences, too, and we tightened up the wire where it was needed, replaced a few rotting posts, and branded more cattle in the next few days. He'd been working up Montana way and in the Dakotas and had first come west from Illinois, working on the railroad, building at first, then as a switchman.

It was the sort of story every man had to tell them days. Men moved often and turned their hand to almost anything, developing the knacks for doing things. Most men were handy with tools—their lives demanded it of them—and most men worked at a variety of jobs, usually heading toward a piece of land of their own. Some made it, some never did. In any bunkhouse you'd find men from a dozen states or territories, and men who had worked at dozens of jobs, doing whatever was needed to earn a living.

Most of them were young, and the younger they were the harder they worked to be accepted as men. No boy over fourteen wanted to be thought of as a boy . . . he wanted to be considered a man and a top hand at whatever he was doing.

The first thing he learned was to do his part. Nobody had any use for a shirker or a lay-around . . . it just made more work for the others, and such a one became almighty unwelcome awful fast. On the other hand, nobody asked who you were or where you came from, only that you stood up when there was something to be done.

Nobody thought of horses except as companions and working partners. The value of a horse in terms of money wasn't often mentioned. You'd hear a man say, "He's a damn' fine cuttin' horse." Or maybe, "He'll go all night an' the next day. Stays right in there." Or, "That's the horse I rode when I tied onto that brindle steer that time, an' . . ."

You hear folks say how horses were rough used on old-time ranches, but it ain't so. At least, they used them no worse than they used themselves, and usually a whole sight better. You'll hear folks say that horses are stupid, but they ain't if you give them a chance. A horse is like a dog . . . he needs to belong to somebody, to be trusted by somebody. Once they know what's expected of them they'll come through.

There was no word from Milo Talon, and I lay awake nights wondering what Flanner would do next. Me an' Em talked it over at breakfast, with Al Fulbric putting in his two cents' worth. The result was that I got out a team that had once been broke to harness, hitched them to a plough, and then went out and ploughed a firebreak twelve furrows wide just below the crest of the hill that divided us from town. It taken several days, but I got it done, and Al ploughed some on the other side.

Back up into the woods we scouted the country, and here and there tied onto a dead fall and dragged it into place. In other places we cut trees and felled them so they'd form a barrier to riders or even men on foot. We laid out trails through these barriers with certain logs to be lifted to let us by. It was like one of these mazes you hear tell of. If a man knew his way as we did he could ride through almighty fast, but if he didn't know the key entrance and exit he played hob gettin' through.

Fire was what we feared most. We set out barrels and filled them with water near the barns and bunkhouse, and we shot more meat and jerked it against a long fight.

Two nights later I woke up with a yell ringing in my ears. Somebody was pounding on the door and yellin' "Fire!" I grabbed for my hat and my pants, slamming the first on my head and scrambling into the others. I stamped my feet into boots, grabbed my gun belt, and ran for the door.

The whole horizon was lit by flames. They were coming right at us with a good beat of wind behind them. As I ran for the corral I heard the beat of hoofs and Al Fulbric came out on the dead run. He was in his long johns with a gun belted on, waving his rifle and yellin' like a Comanche. But across his horse in front of him he had a bunch of old sacks and a spade.

It taken me a moment to throw the leather on the roan and get into the saddle. There were sacks laid out and ready and I grabbed a bundle along with a shovel and raced after him.

We reached our firebreak just ahead of the flames. Believe me, had it not been there we'd have been wiped out, but because it was lyin' like it was, on our side of the hill, Flanner hadn't even guessed it was there.

We hit the dirt, and leaving our horses on the ranch side of the break, we ran across and went to whipping out the first inroads of flame with our sacks. We managed to fight it for a bit, then fell back after starting backfires.

The backfires burned right up to our firebreak and gave us about fifty more feet of leeway. Only a few sparks managed to blow across to the ranch side and we whipped those out or buried them with earth before they got started.

Pennywell was right there with us, and so was Em. Suddenly I turned sharp around. "The house!" I said. "They've gotten into the house by now!"

We hit our saddles on the run, Em no slower than the rest of us, and we went down the slope on the run.

As we came into the back door, a bunch of men were crowdin' into the front door and Em ran through, me behind her. Al cut around through another room.

Len Spivey was there, and Matthews, and some others. Len was grinning. "Looks like we got you! Jake thought that fire would do it."

They all had guns in their hands and there were eight of them and only two of us in sight.

They guessed right on some things, they guessed wrong on Emily Talon.

"You got nothing," she said, and she cut loose her dogs . . . only they were slugs from a big Dragoon Colt.

They couldn't believe it. They'd been sure if there was trouble it would come from me, and they paid no mind to the womenfolks, or mighty little. And they didn't even know about Al.

Em just tilted her old pistol and cut loose, and just as she fired, Al Fulbric jumped from the bedroom door with a shotgun in his hands, and somehow my old six-shooter was speaking its piece right along with them.

It was shock that won for us. They'd not expected shooting with the women there, not really knowing what kind of a woman Em was. It was shock and the time it takes a man to react. Em's first shot caught Matthews, who was closest to her, and turned him halfway around. His own gun went off into the floor just as Al cut loose with a double-barreled shotgun.

Matthews was falling, shot through the body. Another man grabbed at the doorjamb and slid down it to the floor, and Len Spivey threw himself at the door and damn near broke his neck getting out of there.

We ran to the door after them. One man turned to fire and my bullet cut him right across the collarbone from side to side. I saw him stagger and cry out, seen his shirt flop where the bullet cut it, and then I put a second one into his brisket. And then they were gone.

They left three behind. Matthews was down and dying. The man who slid down the doorjamb had taken a load of buckshot at twelve-foot range, and he was dead. A third man lay on the grass outside the front door.

They'd drawn us off with the fire as they figured, but they had guessed wrong on Emily Talon.

I might have held back myself, for fear of the women getting shot, but there was no hold-back in Em.

Nor in Pennywell.

She had got off two shots. I saw her loading up again afterwards. She was pale as a ghost when it was over, but she was thumbing two cartridges back into her pistol, and she was ready.

Man, those were *women!*

12

There was a meanness in me. We'd come off lucky. Em had been burned by one bullet, but that was the only injury to any of us.

We'd lost some grass, but spring rains and the winter snows would bring that back. The burning left us secure from that side at least, for now there was nothing left to burn.

They'd busted through the front window. They'd tried to break down the door, but it just didn't bust that easy. They'd pried off one of the shutters and had busted through the window to get in. That was what allowed us time to get down there.

But it was not in me to sit by, so I went right outside, and saying nothing to anybody I hit the road for town. I pulled up in the shadow of a barn, saw their horses at the hitch rail of the hotel-saloon, and I walked across the street and up the steps. They were all inside, cursing and swearing and downing drinks when I came through the door, and they turned around thinking I was Flanner.

I never said yes or no, I just cut loose. My first bullet

taken Len Spivey just as he closed his fist over his gun butt. It slammed him into the bar and the second one opened a hole right in the hollow at the base of his throat.

One other man went down before a slug hit me in the leg and I started to fall. I braced myself against the wall, hammered the rest of my shells into them, and then commenced pushing the empties out.

The room was full of smoke from that old black powder, and from somewhere near the bar flame stabbed at me and I was hit again.

I didn't fall. I just kept plugging fresh cartridges into those empty chambers and then lifted my six-gun for another have at them. Sliding down the wall to one knee I peered under the smoke that filled the room. I saw some boots, stabbed two shots about four feet above them, and saw a man fall.

I crawled toward the door and managed to push it open and get outside. Nobody needed to tell me I was hard hit, and nobody needed to tell me I'd done a damn fool thing to ride into the enemy camp and go to blasting.

My horse was yonder, and I crawled for him. A door opened in the side of the hotel, then closed easy like. I hitched myself down the steps into the street and using the hitch rail, pulled myself to my feet.

I was backing across the street, gun in hand, when Jake Flanner stepped around the corner of the hotel on those crutches of his. He had a six-shooter in one hand, and he kind of eased his weight on the other crutch and lifted the gun. At the same moment I saw Brewer come out of the saloon door. He had a rifle in his hands and he was maneuvering himself into position for the kill.

My gun came up. I took a step back and my boot came down on a rock that rolled under it. Weak as I was, it was all that was needed. The stone rolled, I staggered and fell just as two guns went off, followed quickly by a third.

That last had a different sound. It was a sharper *spang,* not the dull report of the forty-four. I saw Brewer stagger and go down, then crawl around the corner and out of sight.

Flanner was gone. An instant ago he was there and then he was gone.

I started to get up and felt a hand under my arm. "Easy now!" The voice was strange, but my eyes were fogging over and when I started to look around he said, "You'll have to walk. I can't carry you and shoot. Let's go."

Somewhere along in the next few minutes I felt myself getting into a saddle, and I felt the movement of a horse because every time he set a hoof down it hurt like hell.

There was a fire burning. I liked the pinewood smell. It was night and there was a roundup of stars right overhead. I could see them through the branches of a tree. My head ached and I didn't feel like moving, so for a long time I just lay there looking up at the stars.

After a while I must have passed out again because when my eyes opened the sky was gray and there was only one star left on the range of the sky. For a time I lay there looking at it and then my eyes located the fire. It was down to coals and gray ash, and over beyond it I could hear that wonderful sound of horses munching grass.

Nothing moved so I just lay there, not even wondering what had happened to me or where I was. Then I smelled something else and my eyes located it, a blackened coffeepot on the coals.

I wanted coffee. I wanted it bad but I wasn't so sure I could get to it or what I'd drink it out of. For a while I lay there, listening to the wind in the pines, and finally it began to come over me that I'd been shot . . . I'd been hit at least once, probably twice or more. Somehow I'd gotten out of town. Vaguely, I recalled a gentle voice and a hand on my arm. I recalled riding, and a hand on me

much of the time. Finally I'd been tied into the saddle
. . . but where was I now?

When I made a try at moving my right arm I found it
was tied up somehow. My left was free.

Reaching out, my hand encountered something . . . my
pistol! Well, I'd been left a gun, anyway. I could see the
horses now, right yonder beyond a few scattered aspen.
They were picketed and eating grass. Turning my head
I saw somebody sleeping off on my left. His head was on
a saddle, and he was bundled up in blankets with part
of a ground sheet over him . . . but it was no type of
ground sheet I'd ever known.

My right arm was hurt. Rolling to my left side a little
I pushed into a sitting position. The horses looked over
at me. There were two horses, one of them my roan.

Some gear was stacked on the grass near us, and two
packsaddles. So this gent was a drifter. His gear looked
a whole lot better than any drifter I'd ever come across,
and he hadn't much in the way of spurs on his boots . . .
and they weren't western boots.

When I started to twist a little I got a shot of pain
through me that made me gasp, and when I gasped this
sleeping man came awake sudden-like.

He was a tall man, not more than thirty, and handsome.
He was one of the best dispositioned men I ever met, and
he dressed neat. His outfit was all of the best, and while
I couldn't make out his rifle, it was a handsome weapon.

He sat up and looked over at me. "Don't try moving,"
he said, "you'll start bleeding again. I had a hard time
getting it stopped."

"Where'd you come from?"

He chuckled dryly. "What does it matter? I came at
the right time, didn't I?" He shot me a look. "What happened in there, anyway?"

"We had us a fight. They were pushing us hard so I
decided to push back. I done it."

"Did you get any of them?"

103

"I got two inside. I thought I got another outside, or somebody did."

"That was me. I took a shot at the man with the crutches but missed. Probably it was just as well. I'd hate to shoot a crippled man."

"Just because a man's got game legs doesn't say he's got a good disposition. That was the worst of the lot. That was Jake Flanner."

"What was the fight about?"

"Ranch out yonder," I said, "called the Empty . . . for MT. There's an old lady runnin' it . . . salt of the earth . . . named Emily Talon. Those back in Siwash were tryin' to run her out, and I got myself into the fight . . . I don't exactly know how. They hit us, tried to burn us out, and we saved the ranch, then whipped them in a fight at the house. But they'd be coming again and I got sore, them pushing an old lady that way . . . so I rode into town."

"Alone?"

"Why not? There wasn't all that many of them. And I couldn't take from them the only hand they've got."

"You look familiar."

"There's a few posters around. My name is Sackett. Logan Sackett."

"Hello, cousin. I am Barnabas Talon. Em is my mother."

Lying back on my blankets, I looked him over. He had the look, all right. He reminded me of Em, and a little more of Milo. "Heard you were in England."

"I came back. We'd received word a few years ago that ma was dead and buried. We were notified of it, and that the estate had been settled. There seemed no reason to return, so I kept on with what I was doing.

"A few months ago I was talking about Colorado with some English friends, and they commented on seeing the house, our house, and they had heard about an old woman who lived there alone.

104

"At first I thought it was nonsense, but it worried me, so I caught a ship and came over. In New Orleans I went to an old man who had been pa's attorney, and he told me there had been no settlement of the estate and that he had a letter from ma not two months before. So I started home."

He filled a cup with coffee and handed it to me. "My father taught me caution. I had been formally notified that the estate had been settled and ma was dead. Obviously someone had done so for a reason. Apparently the reason was to cause me to forget Colorado and whatever property we had there.

"Whoever had such intentions would not be pleased if I returned, so I came quietly, and when I reached Denver, I made inquiries. Nobody knew anything until I consulted a former deputy sheriff whom I knew. He told me that a man named Jake Flanner, who had lived in Siwash, was hiring fighting men . . . the worst kind.

"There had been a mention of a man named Flanner in ma's last letter to me, so I came along through the country passing myself off as a mining engineer. I was warned a couple of times I'd better go somewhere else, that the area around Siwash was headed for trouble.

"Just as I was riding into town you fellows cut loose in there, and when you came out I got a good look at you in the light over the door. I could see you'd been hit and you were favoring one leg, but you were still in there with that six-shooter. Then Brewer came out and he started to pull down on you so I shot him, then flipped a quick one at that crippled man."

"How'd you get my horse?"

"You told me where it was."

Well, I remembered none of that. Seems I told him some other things, too.

"You'd better keep an eye on our back trail," I warned him. "They won't give up."

"You forget that I grew up around here. I know hiding

places in these hills they'd take years to find. I knew places that even pa never knew. Only Milo and me."

"I put out word for him. If he hits the outlaw trail they'll tell him."

He looked at me. "Milo? An outlaw?"

"Not really, I guess. It's just that they all know him. And he's got a way with that gun of his."

Lying there alongside the fire I told him about Em, Pennywell, and the place. I also told him about Albani Fulbric, bringing him up to date on the situation.

By the time I'd finished I was all in. I drank a swallow more of coffee and eased myself back on the blankets. It was broad daylight and I could see Barnabas was worried.

"You better mount up and head for the Empty," I said. "They'll know they put lead into me and they'll try to get to the ranch."

"I can't leave you," he said. He squatted on his heels. "Logan, I got to tell you. You're hit very hard. You took three slugs. One went through the muscles on your upper leg, and you got another one in the upper arm, but the bad one is through the body. You've lost a lot of blood." He paused a moment. "I am not a physician, but I do know a good deal about bullet wounds. I was an officer in the army of France for a while during the war with Prussia. I can't leave you."

"You'd better. Em will need you. As for me, it's going to be a long, hard pull."

He looked at me for a long time, then he went to his pack and got out some coffee and other grub which he stached near me. He refilled my cartridge belt, and broke out a box of forty-fours. "Lucky I had these. I bought them in case they were needed on the ranch."

He squatted on his heels again. "You're about six or seven miles back of the ranch, but there's no short way across. It will take me most of the day to get there.

"Right down there is the spring. Your canteen is full

and I'm leaving mine also. There's a big pot of coffee, and I'll try and get some help to you as soon as I see how it is on the ranch."

I looked around at the hills. It looked like a cirque, or maybe a hanging valley. It was a great big hollow that was walled in on three sides, or seemed to be, and maybe three hundred acres in the bottom of it. There were a lot of trees, and there probably was a lake . . . in such formations they were frequently found.

Barnabas saddled up, looked down at me once more, then rode off. And I was alone.

For a while I just lay there. The sun was in the hollow and the shadows of the aspen leaves dappled the grass with shadow. I was weak as a cat, and I just lay there resting.

How much of a trail had Barnabas Talon left? He might be a good man on a horse and with a gun, yet he could have left sign a child could read. Covering a trail is an art, and far from a simple one. I've heard of folks brushing out tracks with a branch. That's ridiculous— the marks of the branch are a sign themselves. Anything like that must be done with great care to make it seem the ground has not been disturbed by anything. A tracker rarely finds a complete track of man or beast on a trail he's following. Only indications of passage.

The spring was all of thirty yards off, but there was no flat ground nearer on which a man could sleep. It was all rocks down there. With my rifle close at hand and my horse nibbling grass a few yards away, I dozed the long day through. Come evening I added a few sticks to the fire, poured some water into a pot Barnabas left, shaved some jerky into it, added some odds and ends, and set it on the fire. Then I just lay back and rested.

You want to know something? I was scared. I never feared man nor beast when I was on my feet with two good hands, but now I was down, weak as could be, and my right arm was useless.

Later, I ate my stew and contemplated. I had no idea Barnabas Talon would get back. He would intend to, but there'd be need of him there and his first duty was to his ma. As for me it would be root hog or die, so I settled to figuring what I could do.

My chances were slim if Flanner's men trailed me down, as they would surely try to do. Despite what Talon said, I'd no doubt they could find this place, so I must find a better one . . . somewhere I could really hide.

My need for water tied me to the spring, so I commenced to study the ground, looking for someplace I could hide. There were tumbled boulders down the stream bed below the spring, and scattered branches of dead trees, piled-up rubble, and debris.

When I finished my stew, and mighty good it tasted, I took a long pull at a canteen and felt better.

Yet worry was upon me. There was weakness in me, and I'd an idea the worst was yet to come, that I might become so weak I could not move, even delirious. I'd seen men gunshot before this and knew my chances were slight if caught in a sudden shower with a fever upon me. And showers in the high peaks are a thing that happens almost every day.

I saw nothing that would help. No caves, no corners hidden from the wind . . . nothing.

Suppose I crawled into the saddle and made a try for the ranch? I'd never make it, of course. And my horse was not saddled now, and there was no way I could get a saddle on it. Yet there had to be a way.

Gathering my gear together, I rolled my bed, drank the last of the coffee, and using my rifle pulled and pushed myself up until I stood on one foot, clinging to an aspen. Inch by careful inch I searched the terrain. There was little I'd not seen in my few years and I knew about all that could happen to trees, brush, and rocks that would provide a place to hide, and I found none of it here.

Yet there was something nagging at me, something I

should notice, something that worried at my mind like a ghost finger poking me. No way my thoughts took brought any clue to mind, and one by one I climbed the trees of my ideas and looked over the country around each of them. But I came upon nothing.

It came to me at last as I was hitching myself along from tree to tree toward the roan.

What I heard was a waterfall.

13

Em Talon peered through the slats of the shutter toward the gate. Nothing in sight.

Logan should have returned by now. It was foolish of him to ride off as he had done, yet she knew how he felt, and she also subscribed to the theory that once you have an enemy backing up you must stay on top of him. "Never let them get set," she muttered.

The sky was overcast, the air still. Sullen clouds gave a hint of rain.

She went from window to window, checking the fastenings on the shutters. Pennywell had been up on the lookout atop the house and now she returned. "There's nobody, Aunt Em. The road's empty all the way to town."

"He should be back." She was talking half to herself. What would he have done? Riding in like that? She knew exactly, because it was what she would do. He had tackled them head on, horn to horn. Logan might not be the smartest Sackett there was but he was meaner than a cornered wolf, and he wasn't a back-shooter.

She pictured the town, tried to think out what he would

do. And if wounded? He'd run for the hills. He would try to lead them off, like a wounded quail would do, anything to keep the enemy away from the nest. It was the instinctive response of a wild thing.

He would ride into the mountains, hunt him a hole, and wait until the time was right to come home. If he could get home.

That was the worrisome part, for he might be holed up yonder in the mountains, needing help, needing it the worst way. And the trouble was to pick up his trail a body would about have to pick it up from town, from Siwash.

Pennywell would be no good on a trail of that kind; besides, she was vulnerable. She was a young thing, and it would not do for her to be traipsing around the hills with the kind of men around that Flanner had brought into the country.

Al? She hesitated. He might be a good man on the trail, but he was new to this country, and trailing was more than a matter of following the sign a body found.

She did know the country, and she could read sign as good as any Sackett she knew of, which was better than most.

Em Talon made up her mind, and she made up her mind there was nothing to do but get ready. There was also a matter of time. She'd have to cut out from the ranch at a time when she'd not be seen, she'd have to get up there in the hills and find Logan.

She told them over breakfast. "I'll be gone a day or two. Al, you stay here an' take care of the place an' you watch over Pennywell."

"Ma'am," Al Fulbric protested, "you just cain't do that! You ain't a young woman, and those are mighty rough mountains."

"Of course, they're rough! That's why I like 'em. Son, I'm mountain born an' bred. I growed up walkin' the hills. I run a trap line before your mammy was born. As for these here hills, I've dodged Injuns all over them. I know the hideouts, and I know the mind of a dodging Sackett.

"We don't run just like other folks do, an' I know what Logan'll do, more than likely. You leave him to me. Just ketch me up that grulla mule out yonder—"

"Mule?"

"That's right. Him an' me been to the wars together, an' we can go again."

"If you say so, ma'am. A mule's not very fast."

"Neither am I. But I know that there mule and he'll take me there and bring me back, and that's what counts at my age, mister."

"Yes, ma'am. At any age."

Al walked out the back door and to the corral. He looked at the mule doubtfully and the mule looked at him. "I'd like to have this friendly," Al said. "It's the old lady's idea, not mine."

The mule put his ears back, and Al shook out a loop. He had tried to rope mules a few times, and had done it too . . . after a while. Most of them had a gift for ducking a rope. He walked out into the corral trailing his loop and studying the situation.

Behind him he heard Emily Talon. "You won't need that rope. Coley, come here!"

Without hesitation, the mule walked right to her. She fed him a carrot and slipped the halter on him while Al Fulbric gathered his rope.

"What was that you called him?"

"Coley . . . it's short for his name. Coleus. Talon named him, and Talon was a reader of the classics. The way he tells it, Coleus of Samos was the first Greek to sail out of the Mediterranean into the Atlantic."

"Well, I'll be! What did he want to do that for?"

"Seems some other folks—the Phoenicians, it was, who

111

were some kin to the Philistines of the Bible—they had that whole end of the Mediterranean sewed up. They had laid claim to all that range, and they let nobody sail that way.

"This Coleus, he told them he got blown that way by a storm, and anyway he got through the Gates of Hercules and out into the Atlantic. And then he sailed up to Tartessus and loaded his ship with silver. That one trip made him a rich man.

"Talon favored him because he done the same. Folks said he was crazy to ride out here and start ranching in country only the Indians wanted. Anyway, Coley here, he had a way of straying into new pastures hisself, so Talon named him."

"I like it." Al Fulbric spat into the dust. "A man like that deserves credit."

"After that trip he never needed credit. He could afford to pay cash. Anyway, that's how Coley come by his name, and we've come a fur piece together, Coley an' me. We've been up the crick and over the mountain, and he'll fight anything that walks."

"That *mule?*"

"That mule, as you call him, was a jack once. They cut him, but they done forgot to tell him about it. He still figures he's a jack, and don't you borrow no trouble from him or he'll take a piece out of you."

Em Talon picked up her saddle and before Al could move to help her, had slung it in place and was cinching up. She slid her Spencer into the boot, then turned on him.

"Al, you go about your business now. I'm goin' to ride him astride, which no decent woman ought to do, but I'll have no man standin' by when I do it. You get to the house and keep a sharp lookout. They'll be a-comin', especially if they got Logan."

Al swore, spat into the dust, and walked off toward the house. When he reached the steps he turned to look back.

Em was riding out toward the gate, and sure enough, she was sitting astride, and he could see a short stretch of her long-johns where they disappeared into her boot tops.

He blushed a little and turned his head away, ashamed for what he had seen. Pennywell was pouring coffee when he entered the house.

"She beats me," he said, "she really does. I'd have gone—"

"She'd not let you, and one thing I've learned about Em Talon, Al Fulbric, and that is that you get no place arguing with her. She's a notional woman, but the only notion she pays mind to is her own. When she sets her mind to something, you just stand clear."

Emily Talon was no longer young, but there was a toughness in her hard, lean body that belied its age. She had never been one to think in terms of years, anyway. A person was what they were, and many a man at forty was sixty in his ways and many another was twenty and would never grow past it.

As a small girl she had helped her father and brothers with their trap lines, and when she was ten she had one of her own. She was more familiar with the life of the forest than of the settlement, and riding away from the ranch she suddenly felt free, freer than she had felt in many a year.

She scouted back of the town, between Siwash and the hills. A Sackett hurt and hunted was a Sackett heading for the high up yonder. She knew their nature well for she was one of them . . . he would ride out and he would ride far.

As it was getting dark she came upon a trail, only it was two horses rather than one. Puzzled, she studied the tracks again. One of them had to be the roan . . . and the roan seemed to be led.

She squinted at the tracks warily, then looked all around. Nobody seemed to be watching, nobody seemed

113

to have followed them, yet all hell must have torn loose down there in town.

Scouting farther she saw bunched tracks . . . seven or eight riders, not on the trail of the two, but hunting it.

She had to have more information, so she rode toward town. It was dark, and she was unlikely to be seen, but she knew where to go.

There had been a time when men had killed over Dolores Arribas, but the years had gone by and somehow she had found herself at the end of a trail in Siwash.

In her veins was the blood of Andalusia, but there was Indian blood, too, the blood of a people who built grandly in stone when Spain was only the hinterland of Tarshish.

She washed the clothes of the gringo but took no nonsense from him. Fiercely proud, she walked her own way in the town, unmolested, even feared.

Emily Talon knew that of all the people in Siwash, Dolores would know what had happened and that she would be willing to tell what she knew.

The mule picked his way delicately up the alleyway and around to the dark side of the stable. Em did not dismount, for Dolores Arribas was sitting on her steps in the cool of the evening, watching the clouds.

"You ride very late, Mrs. Talon." She spoke with only the trace of an accent.

"There was a shooting in town?"

"Yes. Two men are dead, two are wounded. One will die, I think." She spoke matter-of-factly, and then added, "They were Flanner's men."

"And he who done the shootin'?"

"There were two . . . one of them was Logan Sackett, but Jim Brewer was killed by another man, a stranger with a rifle, a tall, elegant man."

"Logan was hurt?"

114

"Yes . . . he was hit very hard . . . more than once. The other man took him away."

"I got to find them."

"You think you are the only one? Flanner looks for them, too. At least, his men look for him."

They were silent, and then Dolores suggested, "You would like a cup of tea? It is long, the way you will ride."

"I reckon. Yes, I'll take that tea."

She got down from the mule, spoke gently to it, and followed Dolores into the house. It was a small house, and even in the darkness she could feel its neatness.

"I will not make a light. The water is hot."

"Thank you."

They sat in the vague light, and Dolores poured the tea.

"Where are your sons?"

"I wish I knew. Milo, he's ridin' somewheres, but Barnabas, he went off to Europe, lived right fancy the way I hear tell. I always figured him for that, but wondered why he never wrote. Then I heard. Somebody passed word that I was dead and the place broken up."

"He would do that. It is like him."

"Flanner?"

"Of course. That way they might not bother to come back. What is there for anyone in Siwash? Except those of us who have no money with which to leave."

For a while they sat in silence, then Emily said, "If it's just money—"

"I earn my own money."

"Reckon so. Reckon you always will. I just figured that if a loan would help you to move out of this place, I could come up with it."

"Gracias. I do not think so. I will wait. Soon I will have enough, and then I shall go." She paused. "At least you were never one of those who tried to force me to go."

"No, I never was . . . nor was Talon." Emily Talon hesitated. "It was just that you were too popular, and a

115

durned sight too much woman. They were afraid you'd take their men from them."

"I did not want them." She turned her head and looked at Em in the darkness. "You were not afraid?"

"Of Talon? No . . . one woman was all he ever wanted. One that was his own."

"You are right, but what of your son?"

"Milo? You mean you an' Milo?"

"Not Milo."

"Barnabas? I didn't think he had it in him."

"He was a good man, a fine man. I liked him. He was a gentleman."

"Thanks." Em got to her feet. "I got to be far back in the hills come daylight."

"Be careful. Jake Flanner will not care that you are a woman. Nor will most of the men he has now . . . they are scum."

"I know that Len Spivey. I . . ."

"Do not worry about him. He will not be one of them."

At the door Em paused, looking back. "Len Spivey?"

"Logan killed him. He was the first one."

Em went down the steps with care, then paused to look carefully about. At last she crossed the small yard to the mule. Dolores Arribas, standing in her doorway, heard the leather creak as she mounted.

"Mrs. Talon? I did not see it, but from what I heard I would swear that was Barnabas out there today."

Emily Talon waited a slow minute, wanting to believe it. "Barnabas?"

"He rode in at the right time. They'd have killed Sackett. Oh, he was making his fight, but he'd been hit hard and Jake Flanner himself was lining up for a shot and so was Brewer."

"And Barnabas fetched him?"

"He did. He took Brewer out, then turned his rifle, but Flanner was gone."

"That's Jake, all right. That's Jake Flanner."

116

"Yes, Mrs. Talon. So you be careful. Very, very careful. It is you they want, you know. Just you."

Emily Talon turned her mule toward the mountains. Barnabas was back. Her son was home again.

14

Em Talon was a considering woman, and now she gave thought to Barnabas and his plight. He was riding into the mountains with a wounded man. He would need shelter, and he would need medical attention for Logan. The obvious place was the Empty, but if they had tried to cross the country between Siwash and the ranch they would have certainly been inviting death.

Hence they must have headed for the mountains, to lose themselves in the forest at the earliest possible moment.

Barnabas would undoubtedly try to reach the ranch, but he had never known the mountain trails as Milo had, and Logan might be in no condition to show him the trail he knew. Apparently Barnabas emerged from the gun battle uninjured, but there was no way she could be sure of that.

Talon had hunted and trapped these mountains years before any other white man he knew of, and part of that time Em had hunted with him. She knew trails where no trails seemed to be, and she knew those the buffalo used to find the mountain meadows.

When he was but ten years old she had once taken Barnabas with her into the mountains, showing him the lightning-blazed pine on the shoulder of the mountain that marked the opening of the trail to the crest of the ridge. It was likely he would remember that trail, for it had been their first trip into the mountains together, his first trip into the very high mountains. The mule's memory was good, for he had followed this trail many times and as soon as she turned him toward it, he knew where he was going.

It had changed, of course. The screen of brush that concealed the opening was thicker now, and the grove of young aspens had become sturdy trees in the passing of time, but the trail was there and she followed it swiftly. When she was well back in the forest she dismounted and screening the match with her hands, she studied the trail. There were two horses, one close behind the other, the second one probably led.

She made no attempt to guide the mule. It was almost too dark to see the trail under the trees and the mule could be trusted. At places they skirted the very rim of a canyon, a vast depth that fell away on one side. They climbed steadily.

At last, knowing she could go no farther without seeing their tracks, she got down from the mule at a place she knew. She had camped here before. There was fuel and shelter, and sounds from down the canyon carried easily to this point. Unsaddling the mule, she picketed it and wrapped it up in a blanket, leaning against the flat bole of a tree.

For a long time she remained awake looking at the stars through the trees and letting her tired muscles relax slowly to invite sleep. It was not as easy as it once was. She was old now, and her muscles grew stiff too early in the game. She thought ahead, trying to decide where Barnabas would be apt to stop.

Awakening, she watched a chipmunk nibbling at a seed he had found. For a moment she sat still just enjoying the gray light of morning. The air was damp, and she was surprised to observe that a light rain had fallen during the night without disturbing her.

She got up slowly, led the mule to the little trickle of water that came from a spring under the scarp, and dipped enough water for tea. Back at camp she kindled a fire and brewed a cup, drank it, and saddled up, listening to the sounds from down the canyon. She heard nothing, but she had not expected to. If there was pursuit it would come this morning, and by now they were breakfasting and arguing about what happened the night before. That would give her another hour's advantage.

Now she moved with greater care, studying the trail as the mule moved along. Usually she could pick up the sign well ahead—a track here, a bruised leaf there, the mark left by the edge of a shoe. They had been moving slower; obviously Barnabas was hunting a place to stop.

She rode into the cirque almost an hour later when the sun was halfway up the morning. It was right at timberline, the last of the growth giving way to the tumbled talus of broken rock that had broken off the walls and fallen down to mingle with the stunted growth and grass. She found the place where the horses had cropped grass and crushed down grass and wild flowers where a bed had been.

One rider had ridden off by himself, leaving the other behind. That would be Barnabas heading for the Empty, which was hard to get to from here unless a body knew every twist of the trail.

But where was Logan Sackett?

She knew he had to be in bad shape, and a hunted man in bad shape would hunt a hole. He would want to be out of sight, and he would need water and a place for his horse. Em Talon scanned the country, studying every possible nook or corner that might offer such a shelter. There were several possibilities but all came to nothing.

Logan Sackett had vanished.

Could he have followed Barnabas? It was a possibility. In any event there was one thing she could do. She could make a lot of tracks so those who might try to find him would not guess that he was hidden, as Em was quite sure he was.

Yet the cirque's high walls eliminated any possible way out on three sides. A rider or walker would have to go down the mountain. Mounting her mule again she also turned toward the open side of the cirque and walked the animal down the dim trail into the canyon.

White, slim aspens lined the trail on either side, their pale green leaves trembling slightly. Due to some quirk of temperature or wind currents this grove was higher on the mountain's slope than the aspen was usually found. The grove was littered with the long dead trunks of fallen trees, remnants of some old landslide or snowslide. She was well into the grove when she heard a sound of horses.

Drawing rein, she listened below her, below on the trail she had herself followed into the cirque.

A moment later they came into view. There were eight men, all tough men by their look. The man in the lead was Chowse Dillon, occasional cowpuncher, occasional outlaw, consistent troublemaker. They were no more than a hundred and fifty yards right down the hill, a hill too steep for a horse to climb except on the switch-back trail they followed. Yet by the trail they must follow they were a half mile away.

Em lifted her rifle and put a bullet into the dust about a foot in front of Dillon's horse. Most of the riders were undoubtedly on broncs—she had counted on that. The sudden *spat* of the bullet as well as the thunder of the heavy rifle in the confinement of the rock walls was enough.

Dillon's horse reared straight up, spinning halfway around to bump the horse behind. Instantly horses were buck-jumping all over the narrow trail and one of the horses went over the edge, rider and all, rolling into the trees and deadfalls below.

Two men unlimbered their six-guns and shot into the trees where she was, but they were shooting blind and hit nothing. The shooting only added to the confusion. Emily

Talon rode calmly on down the trail she had been following, leaving them cursing and fighting their horses.

The trail was never more than four or five feet wide. Somebody was up there with a rifle and willing to dispute the trail, and nobody was eager to be the first to accept the challenge.

Yet she had ridden scarcely a quarter of a mile, winding down a steep trail, when she picked up the first sign since leaving the cirque. It was the white scar left by a glancing blow from a shoe, and it was fresh! She tried listening for the horses of the men she had seen on the trail but she could hear nothing but the tumbling waters of a nearby fall.

Em Talon did not like the place. She did not like any place that drowned the sounds from her ears. She wanted to hear . . . she needed to hear.

The falls was about eight feet wide, a fairly thin sheet of water except at bottom where it plunged among some boulders and slabs of rock. There it was a thick white burst of foaming water that then plunged off down the mountain in a series of steep cascades.

At the top of the falls trees leaned over the stream, and near the base was a mass of fallen timber, trees washed down from above, some of them with masses of roots, leaving a veritable maze.

Emily Talon contemplated her situation. Somewhere up the mountain behind her were several of Jake Flanner's men, and down at the ranch Barnabas, the son she had not seen in years, was returning home or trying to. Neither Pennywell or Al knew him, and they were just as apt to shoot as not.

Suddenly Em decided there was but one thing to do. She had to get off the mountain and back to the Empty. If Logan was anywhere about he was well hidden, too well hidden to be found while she herself was hunted. She hesitated a moment, but the mule was tugging at the reins, wanting to go on down the mountain, and she gave in.

121

At that moment she was less than seventy yards from Logan Sackett and he was looking right at her, trying to call. But he was too weak. His hoarse shouts could not be heard above the noise of the falls. Em Talon rode on.

15

There I lay, weak as a cat and scarce able to crawl, and I seen that ol' woman draw up there and look down toward me. She was lookin' right square into my eyes, only I was behind the falls and could not be seen. I tried to yell out, but I could scarce make a sound louder than a frog croaking, and she heard nothing.

That she was huntin' me I had no doubt, and in the shape I was in I dearly wanted to be found. Yet she kept turning to look back up the trail and that made me wonder. A short time back I'd been asleep and something waked me. It could have been a shot, although behind that falls even a shot was muffled. Yet something on her back trail worried her, and she rode on.

Looked to me like I'd covered all sign, all right, but I'd done it too durned well. There was every chance I'd die right here, and nobody would find me or know what happened. Well, I'd not be the first western man that happened to. Many a man rode off them days and never came back . . . there was a sight of things could happen to a man that had nothing to do with guns or Indians or anything like that.

A man could get throwed from his horse and die of thirst, or he could drown swimming a river, get caught in a flash flood, fall off a cliff, get bit by a rattler or a hydrophoby skunk, or cut himself with an ax. A lot of men them days traveled alone and worked alone, and if they had an accident that could be the end of them.

I'd known of three men who amputated their own legs, and a half dozen who had trimmed fingers off their own hands. There wasn't no medical corps around like there'd been during the war . . . a body just had to make out as best he could.

Now this place I'd found wasn't the only one like it. When water falls off a ledge a certain amount of it just naturally kicks back against the wall, and after years have passed that water wears away the rock slow or fast depending on the force of the water and the softness of the rock. Sometimes it will wear away until with the river cutting down from above it cuts through the rock. Then the flow will go under what had been the rim, leaving a natural arch.

The space behind the falls is often small, and in this case it wasn't far from the year when the riverbed would drop. In other words, I'd lucked out. There'd been a sight more space back there than I reckoned.

Nor was I the first to use it. Pack rats had been back there, and judging by some old droppings, a bear had holed up there one time. Getting to it had been a puzzle, but I'd found a way through the maze of old tree trunks, broken branches, hanging streamers of torn bark, and the like, and I led my horse right into it.

That horse didn't much care for it at first, but after a bit he settled down. I was all in, and I dragged my gear into a corner back from the water and laid myself out. By dark I was in bad shape. I felt hot all over and my mouth was dry. I had me something of a fever and knew I was in trouble, bad trouble.

When I saw Em I tried to call out, but she heard nothing and rode on. I was still watching when the first of the riders came into sight. They were almighty cautious, and there was eight of them. Only one of them glanced toward the falls, and he didn't seem much interested.

After a bit they rode on. I crawled back after getting a drink and passed out on my blankets.

When I came out of it again it was dark night and all I could hear was the steady roar of the falls. For a time I lay there just staring up into the darkness. My mouth was bone dry and I desperately needed a drink but lacked the energy to get over to the falls. I probably would have lay still like that forever, but it was thinking of my horse that got me to move. That horse needed to be let loose. He'd had water but nothing to eat in hours, and I might die right here with that horse tied up.

After a while I rolled over and kind of eased myself to my knees and crawled to the water. I drank and drank, and then I crawled to the horse and, catching hold of a stirrup, I pulled myself up and untied the bridle reins. Then I tied them loosely to the pommel. "You go ahead, boy," I said hoarsely. "You go on home."

You know that horse wasn't about to go? He stayed right there until I led him to the trail's opening and hit him a slap across the rump. Even then he lingered, but I'd slumped down beside the rocks. The last thing I'd done was to swing my saddlebags off the horse and let them fall to the ground.

After the horse had gone I sort of crawled back to my bed and let go of everything. It was gray light with dawn when I first opened my eyes again and I lay there knowing I had to do something. I had to think it out first, then make every move count so that my strength would last. First thing was to get a fire going. The next thing to heat water, bathe my wounds, and make some coffee. There was almighty little in my saddlebags but there might be enough to help.

There was no end of dry wood back of that fall. Some of it was driftwood, but the pack rat's nest was a bundle of dry stuff right at hand. Bundling some of it together

124

I struck a light and got a fire going. It looked almighty good just to have it there, and once it got started I just sort of lay there and stared at it.

After a while I got into my saddlebag and got out an old pint cup I'd been toting around for years. I put water into it and then dumped in some coffee and let it come to a boil. When it had boiled enough to have body to it, I taken it off the fire and sipped a little here and there, trying not to burn my lips. That coffee surely hit the spot, and I started to perk up. After I'd emptied the cup, I boiled more water in it and set to work on those wounds I'd picked up.

Being a big, healthy sort of man I could shed hurts as well as most, better than a lot. I'd lost blood a-plenty, but what I needed now was to check out those wounds for infection. And there seemed to be none. When I'd bathed them pretty well and done the best I could dressing them, I laid back on my blankets and was soon asleep.

When I awakened I felt better. But I was worried about Em Talon. I was fearful that she'd not gotten home safe, and worried about those eight men back-trailing my horse. When that horse came up to the ranch they would think surely I was dead. Barnabas knew where he'd left me, but Em had been right there and she would have found nothing.

I checked over my guns and made ready for trouble, if trouble came. And of one thing I could be sure—where I was, trouble was not far away, dogging my heels all the way to perdition.

It was cold and damp, and for a few minutes I lay still just thinking and listening. My mouth was dry, and I felt almighty hot and tired. Although I was feeling better than I had the night before, there was just no strength in me, not even to build me a fire. I just lay there, staring into the half darkness of the cave and wondering whether

I'd ever get out of there alive. Right then I wouldn't have bet any money on it.

I could hear no sound above the tumbling water, and soon I dozed off again. When I awoke I was hot and dry like before, only more so. My mite of fire had gone out long ago and I poked sticks together and got hold of some old, dry bark from one of them; crumbling it in my hands and striking a match I coaxed a little flame to burning again.

For a while I just poked sticks into the blaze and tried to get some coals, then I put some coffee into the cup again and when it was brewed, I drank it down. Just having something hot inside me felt good.

By now most of them must have figured me for dead. I guessed I had been holed up a couple of days and nights, although it could be longer. I had to get out of this place. I had to get out in the sunlight and the air, and I had to get myself some grub. Without a horse I was going to play hob gettin' anywhere, but I could surely try. If I was to die I wanted to be out in the fresh sunlight and under the trees.

It taken some time, but I rolled my blankets, taken up my guns, and crawled for the opening, dragging my gear along.

When I first got into the air everything looked wrong-side to. It was morning time and I had been sure it was afternoon. Somewhere I'd lost some time . . . a day was it, or two days? By the way my stomach felt it might have been a week.

I studied the trail that I crawled along and I found no tracks. It had rained since I'd come in, but that wasn't surprising as in the high-up mountains it can rain every afternoon and often enough does just that. Whatever tracks there might have been were washed out, and I found the same thing on the regular trail when I got to it —that trail Em had followed showed nothing at all of her mule, those who chased her, or me.

Using the low limbs of a tree I pulled myself up, favoring myself not to open my wounds, and I hitched along the trail, making no effort to hurry. I just wanted to move along. Where I was headed I surely had no idea, only I was going to come down off the mountain to where I could get some better grub.

I taken rest a-plenty, but by the time an hour was passed I'd made more'n a half mile. The river was off to my left, and a mite of a stream was flowing in from the right to join it. I stopped, laying flat out on the grass, and drunk my fill. Then I hobbled on again.

Once, afar off, I seen a deer. And a couple of times grouse flew up, or some bird resembling them. Marmots, of course, were there wherever I came up to a rock pile of some sort. After a while I just couldn't make it any farther and I moved back into the trees and found a place at the edge of a small clearing where I could stretch out in the sun. When I'd rested there awhile, I started on, keeping off the trail and taking time a-plenty. Little by little I worked my way along the mountainside toward the higher meadows back of the ranch.

The easiest way had been to follow along the steep side of the canyon and gradually work my way down. I couldn't travel but a little way without stopping to rest, and nobody was going to see me unless they were looking over into the canyon. Pretty soon the sides grew steeper and I made my way down to the streambed.

It was lucky I did so because the walls became sheer, white rock cut with many places where water had run off or with deep cracks. At the bottom the stream ran almost bank to bank, but there was an edge of sand or gravel that I could work my way along so that I only had to enter the water occasionally for a few steps.

There was a lot of driftwood, logs and such, washed down by the flash floods that happen in mountain country. After a ways I commenced to get awful tired but there was no place to set down. Suddenly I came upon a kind of gap in the wall. It was half filled with trees and such, but beyond it I could see a patch of green that had to be a meadow.

Crawling over the brush in the mouth of the canyon I found myself with a meadow stretching away before me, but I had to wade through marsh to get to dry land. Ahead of me were a bunch of grass-grown hummocks that were old beaver ponds, and higher I could see the still water of beaver ponds that likely had beavers in them yet.

Off to one side there was a grove of aspen, for the beaver never live very far from them. I sat down on a log just inside that aspen grove.

I was beat. My side ached and there was a weakness on me like I'd never felt before. I needed a camp and place where I could lie down and be safe, but the shape I was in I wasn't up to looking around. So I just sat there watching the light change. Huge billows of cloud lifted high above the mountains catching the last light. Slowly I began to peel flakes of thin, very dry bark from a long dead aspen; then I moved off the log with an effort and I began putting a little fire together.

Leaning my rifle against a tree I started cutting ever-green boughs for a bed. The heavy six-shooter on my leg weighted me down, and after a bit I taken it off and hung it on a low branch. Then I went on cutting boughs, rigging me a halfway shelter there in the aspens. Limping back, and nearly played out, I bent over to replenish the fire. I added a few sticks, dropping to one knee to do it. My breath was coming short and my head was dull and heavy. I had started to rise when I heard the footfall on the moss. Just as I started to turn something hit me.

I started to fall, grabbing for my six-shooter, but it was gone. Through a haze of pain I could see the legs of several horses. I tried to get up.

"Hit him." It was Jake Flanner's voice. "Make a job of it."

128

Something did hit me again, and this time I fell flat out on the leaves and grass. And they hit me again and again, only there was no more pain, just the sodden brutality of the blows. The first blow had stunned me, leaving me only a shell.

Somebody kicked me in the side and I felt the warm flow of blood where the wound was torn open. My hand reached out but there was nothing to lay hold of, and after a time I passed out.

It was the rain brought me out of it. A drenching downpour that came down in buckets. The rain brought me to consciousness and to realization of pain, but I did not move. I simply laid there, unable to move, while the rain poured down, soaking me through and through. After a while I passed out again.

They believed they'd killed me for sure this time. That was my first thought, and it stayed with me. Maybe they were right. Maybe I was already dead. Maybe I was dead and this was hell.

I was wet, soaked through, but it was no longer night. It was coming up to morning although there was no sun as yet. As I lay there I began to remember other things. They had shot into me as I lay on the ground. I recalled the roar of the guns and remembered a burning stab of pain. There had been at least three shots . . . funny, how I remembered that.

If they had done that, how was I even alive? How could I realize anything at all? How could I feel? And I did feel. I felt pain, I felt weariness, I felt like just lying there to be finished with my dying. Trouble was, I was mean. Too many folks wanted me dead for me to go out of my way to please them. I opened my eyes and lay there looking at some sodden green-brown leaves and the wet trunk of a tree.

No matter what they'd done or tried to do I was still alive. I knew what was happening to me and a man who can feel is a man who can fight. It just wasn't in me to die there like a dog in the brush without getting some of my own back. Jake Flanner had come after me himself. He'd brought help, but he'd come. And now I was going after him. I'd no idea what happened down there in the valley at the Empty. Nor right at this moment did I care much. I was an animal fighting for life and I tried to roll over to get my hands under me.

I done it. It wasn't easy. I couldn't move at all on one side so I turned over, mighty careful, the other way. I got one hand under me and I pushed up until I could drag a knee up.

As I got to one knee I realized my shirt was stuck to my side where I'd been shot before. I'd been kicked there, right where my wound was, and it had bled some. All right, so I'd lost blood. I'd lost it before this, and a-plenty. They wasn't gettin' no maiden when they tried to bleed me.

I caught hold of an aspen and pulled myself up. By that time there was light enough for me to see what they'd done to me, and it was a-plenty. My shirt front was stiff with dried blood, and so was the side of it. On my left side I found a fresh bullet hole from front to back. The bullet had gone through a place where my shirt bagged out to one side, going clean through without so much as scratching me. I had a fresh scratch atop my shoulder, and I had bruises all over from the blows and kicks. On my skull I had a fresh cut and a couple of lumps.

Oh, they'd laid it to me proper, only being down like I was, lying on soft ground and grass, some of the shock had been taken from the blows. Most of it I had taken, and so I was sore outside as well as inside.

If they'd hunted for my guns in the dark they surely hadn't found them, for there they were—the rifle had fallen from the tree where I'd leaned it and was lying on the wet grass, but the pistol still hung from the stub of a branch where I'd hung it the night before when all weighted down.

My head was throbbing like a big drum, my stomach was hollow and I was weak, but there was a mad on me like nothing I'd ever felt before. Looking around I saw some broken branches, all seasoned and gray from exposure, and out of one of them and a crosspiece of green aspen I fashioned myself a crutch to spare my wounded leg. Then with my six-gun belted on and my Winchester in my good hand, I started off along that trail those riders had left.

It was plain to see where they were going. They were riding down on the back of the Empty, and they were going in for a kill. They had a lead on me, but it wasn't so much. Where they went, I could follow.

My clothes was torn and I looked a sight, but nobody offered me no beauty prizes at any time, so I kept on. My jaw had a healthy growth of whiskers, caked with mud and blood. My hair likewise. Somewhere back along the way I'd lost my hat, and my bloody shirt was ripped in a couple of places, but I was mean as a cornered razorback hog and I was hunting blood.

Here and there at a place where they had to do a switch-back descent, being a-horseback, I just sat down and slid, saving myself some time a-travelin'.

By noontime I could read their sign enough to see I was closing in. They'd stopped a while to wait for sunup, not knowing the trail or what they faced, so I'd gained a mite. As I edged up to the back meadows I expected to hear gunshots, but I heard nothing at all, and that worried me. I didn't want them killing Em Talon, and I knowed that was what they had in mind. And if they killed her there must be no witnesses so they'd kill that girl I'd taken there for shelter. And that was my affair, all mine.

That crutch was sawing into my armpit, making it sore, but I'd no choice. When I slid and crawled down through the rocks near the ranch, I still heard no sound. I could see the horses down in the corral and mine was there. So he'd found his way home, all right. The horse Barnabas

131

rode was there also. He'd gotten into the place alive . . . or at least his horse had.

I'd come to that point of rocks up behind the place and to one side. It was a raw-backed ridge, covered with broken slabs of tilted rocks, a lot of brush, and some scattered pines. There were a thousand hiding places or shelters on that ridge and I could look right into the corrals and yard without being seen . . . I hoped.

The sunlight lay easy upon the yard. The shadows lay where they ought to lie, and the horses lazed in the corrals. There was no sign of horses that shouldn't be there.

I couldn't make it out.

By rights Flanner and his men should have arrived and should have attacked the place. Right now there should be a fight . . . or else Flanner had already taken over. But where were their horses?

It was almost midafternoon and there should be some sign of life around the place. But still nobody showed. With four people on the place somebody should be moving around.

I lay quiet in the brush and studied all the cover around. Maybe the Flanner outfit had moved in, opened fire, and now were waiting, just as I was, for somebody to make a move.

Then I saw something that didn't figure. On the back steps there was a dark patch where no shadow fell. Water would have evaporated in the time I'd been lying there, at least enough of it so's I couldn't see the stain. Water would, but blood wouldn't.

That there was a blood stain.

My side was throbbing so I wrinkled my forehead against it, scowling and squinting. My side was stiff and my whole body was sore. I eased myself down among the rocks, taking a look back and up from time to time. A body can't be too careful, I told myself. Meanwhile I kept my rifle up and ready. Still no move.

Were they all dead? Every last one of them? It didn't

seem likely. But maybe the men were inside now, abusing Em and the rest. That started me worrying, and I figured I had to get down there. Yet suppose they were deliberately keeping quiet, expecting an arrival?

Me?

They'd left me for dead, and if they hadn't believed me dead they'd not have left me at all.

Who, then?

Or was I figurin' it wrong, all wrong?

And while I waited somebody down there might be dead or dying, somebody who depended upon me.

16

The black appaloosa with the splash of white over the right hip had a dainty, dancing step. Even the miles that lay behind had taken none of the spirit from the gelding and he tossed his head at the restraint of the bit, eager to be off and running.

The rider sat erect, holding the reins easy in his hand, a dark and handsome young man whose what-the-hell sort of smile was in odd contrast to the coolness of his eyes.

There had been changes made. Siwash had grown a little, as he could see even from a distance, and despite his seeming ease he rode with cautious eyes on the country. It was unlikely he would be remembered by many . . . quite a few years had passed.

How had Logan Sackett ever gotten into this country? He was a drifter, of course, and his kind might light anywhere. It was odd, now that he thought of it, that he and Logan, who had been friends, might also be kin. He al-

133

ways thought of ma as Em or Mrs. Talon. Somehow he had forgotten she was also a Sackett.

The word had been to avoid Siwash and come right to the ranch, but if trouble lay in Siwash he'd be damned if he'd ride around it.

He stopped in a hollow where the trail passed through an arroyo, and dismounting, brushed off his clothes with care. He combed his hair by running his fingers through it, whipped the dust from his hat, then stepped back into the saddle and rode into Siwash.

Several people saw him ride into Siwash, and one of them was Dolores Arribas. Another was Con Wellington.

Dolores looked once and knew him; Con looked, then looked again. Con swore softly to himself. Logan Sackett and now Milo Talon. Things were looking up around town and he might soon be back in business. One of them— even if Logan was dead, as they believed—would be bad enough, but there was that slim young fellow with the rifle who pulled Sackett out of the soup, and now this one.

Jake Flanner should have left the Empty alone.

Johannes Duckett saw Milo Talon ride in, ride past his livery stable, and tie his horse at the hitch rail. Duckett looked long at that horse. No cowhand could afford a horse like that. Even in this country where there were many horses, such a horse could not be had for love or money.

The rider stepped down and went into the saloon, opening the door with his left hand. Johannes, who knew most of the riders along the outlaw trail at least by name, furrowed his brow with thought. Who was this man? And why was he here? Any outsider might be somebody Jake had sent for, like he had sent for others. The fact that he had gone right to the saloon without putting up his horse might be an indication. Yet it might be otherwise, and Johannes Duckett took up his rifle and walked across the street to the saloon. He entered and went to the bar, keeping the stranger on his left. In his right hand he held

134

his rifle. Johannes Duckett had big, strong hands and he could handle a rifle as easily as a pistol, and often had.

Milo Talon walked right to the bar. "Rye," he said gently, "an honest rye, from the good bottle."

The bartender glanced at him and switched from one bottle to the other under the bar. "Yes, sir," he said. "The good rye. Ain't no better drink," he added.

He waited a minute, let Milo Talon taste his drink, and then said, "Travelin'?"

"Passin' through," Milo said politely. "Ridin' down to Brown's Hole."

"Know the place." The bartender was thoughtful. "Late in the season for much ridin' down thataway. The boys will be pullin' their freight or settlin' down for the winter."

"Maybe I'll do the same," Milo said. He downed the rye, then pointed with his middle finger to a table. "Whatever you have to eat, set it up for me over there . . . the best you have."

"Yes, sir." The bartender looked at him, hesitated, and glanced at the bar. He had seen no money. "These times, when I don't know a man the boss expects cash on the barrel head."

"And rightly so." Milo pointed again with his middle finger. "Over there, and I'm right hungry."

He went outside the door where there was a barrel of water, a wash basin, and soap and towel and washed his hands. When he came in again the bartender was putting food on the table.

Milo sat down, glanced briefly at the long, quiet man at the bar and at the rifle he carried. The man had not ordered a drink. He just stood there, seemingly looking at nothing.

The door opened and two dusty riders walked in and to the bar. "The boss wants you to fix him a hamper of grub. Make it for two days."

"All right." The bartender glanced at Milo, who was eating quietly, showing no interest in the proceedings.

135

Milo glanced up. "Better make it a week's supply," he said gently. "When a man's travelin' an' used to good grub he'll miss it. And he's got a long way to go."

There was a momentary pause, then all eyes turned toward Milo, who continued to eat.

"What's that?" Chowse Dillon turned around. "Who put a nickel in you?"

Milo Talon smiled. "Free advice, offered freely. When a man starts on a long trip he'd better go provided for it. I've always heard that Jake Flanner liked the good things of life. Pack that hamper, bartender, and pack a little grub for those boys, too."

"You tryin' to be funny?"

Milo smiled again. "Of course not, but on a long trip—"

"Nobody said anything about a long trip!" Dillon said irritably.

"Oh, yes, they did. You weren't listening. I mentioned a long trip." Milo finished his coffee and put the cup down gently. "Free advice, freely given. Travel is broadening, gentlemen, and my advice is for you, Mister Flanner, and all concerned to broaden themselves considerably, starting as soon as possible."

They did not know what to make of him. Dillon felt he should be angry but the stranger's manner was mild and he did not seem in the least offensive. Yet there was something in his manner . . . and the fact that he was obviously a seasoned rider.

"I don't know what you're gettin' at," Dillon said. "You're talkin' a lot but you ain't sayin' much."

"Then I shall put it more directly." Milo spoke quietly. "You've been stirring up trouble with the Empty, and we don't like it. So the fun's over, and all you boys who depend on Mister Flanner for a living had better rattle your hocks out of here."

There was a moment of silence. Duckett looked into his glass and said nothing; Dillon was taken aback by the calmness of this stranger, and worried by it. A lot had been happening that he did not like. First there was that other stranger who had pulled in to bail Logan Sackett out of his trouble, and now this man. How many more would there be? When Jake Flanner hired him he had promised it would be an easy job . . . no trouble at all, nobody but an old lady.

Dillon turned to Milo. "You're takin' in a lot of territory, mister. Just who might you be?"

"Milo Talon. Em's my ma, and you boys been makin' trouble for her."

Chowse Dillon was worried. He was no gunfighter, although he'd had a hand in a half dozen shootings, and he had pushed his weight around here and there, mostly against nesters. But there was something about this he did not like at all.

"There's only one of you," Chowse said, trying for a bluff. "You're buckin' a stacked deck."

"Stacked decks don't always turn up the cards a body would expect," Talon said mildly, "especially when I've got all the aces. I didn't come in here to lose anything, and if you'll recall, I opened the game. Of course," he straightened from the bar, "if you boys want to see what I'm holding you'll have to ante up, and the chips are bullets . . . forty-fives, to be exact.

"I'm betting," he said easily, "that I can deal them just a mite faster than you boys can, and without braggin', boys, I can say I ain't missed anything this close since who flunk the chunk."

The bartender was in the line of fire and the bartender had no stake in the game. He worked for Flanner, who paid him well and on time, but a corpse spends no wages. He cleared his throat. "Chowse," he said, "Milo Talon ain't lyin'. What you do is your own affair, but this man is hell on wheels with a pistol. I've heard of him."

Chowse had made up his mind not to push. There were other times, and he could afford to wait. This might be a job for Johannes Duckett, and not for him or the others. Duckett could do it, and he would tell him as much.

There was a coolness about the features of Milo Talon that Chowse did not care for, a coolness somehow belied by the recklessness of his eyes. Chowse Dillon was a stubborn man but he was not an overly brave one. He was dangerous enough when the advantage was his or when backed into a corner, but he had not survived this long without some knowledge of men, and if he read Milo Talon right he was not only a man who would be quick to shoot, but one who would look right into a man's eyes, laugh at him, and shoot him dead.

"I am not goin' to call you," Dillon said. "That's Flanner's affair, if he wants it. If he sends me against you, I'll come, but nothing was said about you."

"He didn't know about me," Milo replied. "Jake Flanner made his bets without having any idea what Em was holding." He chuckled. "Why, ma could whip the lot of you, guns or any other way. You boys just be glad she had that place to watch over and hadn't a free hand to come after you. When I was knee high to a short sheep I saw ma send a bunch of Kiowas packin' . . . and they carried their dead with them."

He stood back from the bar. "Sorry I can't wait to meet Flanner right now, but I'll be back." He paused. "Any of you boys seen Logan Sackett?"

"He's dead." Dillon said it with satisfaction. "Killed right out there in the street. He done tried to take the whole town by himself. And he's dead."

"Where's he buried?"

Dillon's smile faded. "Some other gent who came along helped him off to the hills, but he had lead enough in him to sink a battleship. Come to think of it, that other gent favored you, only he wore store-bought clothes, like a tenderfoot."

"He was no tenderfoot," Milo replied as he backed

toward the door. "That was my brother, Barnabas. I've seen him cut the earlobes from a man at two hundred yards with a Winchester."

He smiled again. "Well, well! Barney is back! Looks to me like you boys bought trouble wholesale! My advice was good," he added from the door, "travel is downright healthy. You boys pull your freight or we'll be back into town to hang everyone among you who isn't killed by bullets."

And then he added, "And don't you count no Sackett dead until you've thrown the dirt on him. I've seen Logan so ballasted with lead you'd never believe a man could carry it and live. But he's alive, which is more than I can say for those who shot him up."

He stepped into the saddle, eyed the door, then gave a quick glance up and down the street. Con Wellington was standing up the street, watching. Con lifted a hand, and Milo waved in return, then rode swiftly from town.

Milo Talon was no fool. He knew what Flanner was attempting, knew also some of the hatred that welled up within the man, and knew he would not easily call it quits. And sheer numbers were always an advantage. He could afford to lose men and still send more into the fight . . . men of that stamp were not hard to find, and there were always renegade Indians.

If Logan Sackett was hurt and holed up in the hills, he must find him. Despite his claims to the contrary ma could not have held out alone for long. It was Logan who had saved her and saved the ranch as well.

The road to the ranch had changed little. Longingly, he waited for his first glimpse of the old house, and when it came he sighed deeply, excited to see it, to find it still standing. He had heard his mother was dead and the land scattered among many owners, but now he knew that story must have been started by Flanner himself in an attempt to keep them away by offering no reason to come back.

Johannes Duckett had stood very quietly at the bar, his beer resting on the polished surface, scarcely tasted. He had listened to Milo Talon, keeping his eyes averted after that first glance. When Milo backed to the door and went out he made no attempt to follow, for he was thinking back to his first days with Jake Flanner.

Flanner had not hired Duckett, merely suggested they ride on together, and Duckett, essentially a lonely man, had done so. Flanner was a talker, an easy, gracious talker who won most of his battles with his smooth tongue. Somehow Flanner always had money, and Duckett, who had more often than not lived from hand to mouth, had found it easier to just ride along with Flanner. Soon Flanner was suggesting things he might do, and Duckett had done them. Occasionally Flanner had said, "Here, you must be short of cash," and then had handed him a twenty, a half dozen twenties, or whatever. Johannes Duckett found himself living better than he had ever lived, and found himself with more ready cash than ever before.

Flanner had not noticed, although he would not have cared, that Johannes Duckett had few needs, but he would have been surprised at the quiet little hoard Duckett had accumulated. A man with few or no wants and a fairly steady flow of cash can gather together a nice sum, and Johannes Duckett accumulated several thousand dollars of which nobody was aware. Neither did they know where Duckett kept it hidden.

Duckett was a lean, quiet man whom some of the hands around Siwash did not consider overly smart. Others who knew him better did believe him smart, but the fact was that the thoughts of Johannes Duckett moved narrowly in only a few deeply grooved channels. He had no particular feelings about good and evil, but he had his own odd compulsions and beliefs. No amount of money or argument could have brought him to kill a child, yet he would have killed a woman without the slightest hesitation, and he had killed several. He had no moral or religious feelings about his, nor could he have explained why he did any of the things he did. He simply had no more scruples about killing a human being than about shooting a snake or a coyote.

He had no loyalty for Jake Flanner, although Flanner believed Duckett followed him from nothing but loyalty. Jake had provided a kind of traveling companion that Duckett liked. He liked Flanner's smooth-talking ways and he liked that Flanner made his life easier. Also, Duckett had decided that Jake Flanner was shrewd . . . he was a winner. And Johannes wanted to be associated with a winner.

Now for the first time he had doubts.

The doubts began when he looked at the great house on the MT. To him it was awesome, astonishing. It seemed impregnable. Emily Talon had seemed the same. In the time before the shooting started he had seen her on the trail or in Siwash and there was something about the gaunt old woman that shook him. When she looked at him he averted his eyes, and had she reason for scolding him he would have stood quietly and accepted it.

Yet he was not one to argue. Had Flanner been less full of his own plans he would have seen that Johannes Duckett was hesitant. Yet the battle had begun, and the time drew on with no decision in view. From time to time Duckett heard gossip around the town about Milo Talon and his brother. A vague feeling of unease worked itself into those deeply channeled furrows within his brain, and for the first time he grew restless.

"Ever been to the western slope?" he asked Flanner once.

"What? No . . . I never have been." Flanner was irritated. "What brought that up?"

"It's a good country, so they say. There's a place named Animas City. Down in a big park around the Animas River."

141

"We've got enough to do right here," Flanner replied. "Why ride away from a sure thing?"

"Is it?"

Jake Flanner was startled. He had become so accustomed to Duckett's ready acceptance of any of his ideas that the comment startled him. "Of course, it is. Once that old woman is out of there we've got the finest setup ever. We'll just move in, and—"

"There's more of them now. There's that girl, and there's Logan Sackett, and now there's that one with the rifle who helped Logan, and some of the boys say there's another man out there."

"Look, Duck, I wouldn't be in this if I didn't know we can win and win big. When the time comes that girl will just go off by herself or one of the boys will take her. And Logan Sackett's dead. No man can soak up the lead he caught without dying. Why, he must have been hit seven or eight times, and as for that other one, I think he caught some lead, too."

"You want to kill that old lady because she busted your knees."

Flanner's face grew red with anger. He stared at Duckett. "All right," he said softly, "I do . . . and I will. But that's beside the case. It is the place we want."

Duckett listened but his thoughts were on this other man . . . Milo Talon. Duckett talked little but he listened a lot, and he knew more about Milo Talon than any other person in Siwash. He knew, for example, that Milo was a lone wolf, that he was amazingly swift and accurate, and that even men known as dangerous avoided him.

The odds were piling up. From now on every shot fired would increase the risk, as there were more people to fire back. Johannes Duckett's thinking was simple. He knew that two and two made four. He also knew that where there had been one old woman on the place in the beginning, although even then some suspected there were more, there were now two women and probably four men, for

142

he had not for a moment accepted Logan Sackett's death. Hurt, maybe, but not dead. Johannes Duckett counted the dead when he saw the bodies.

The odds had risen, and who was to say they would not continue to rise? Sackett was one of the feudal clans from Tennessee . . . who was to say the others might not ride in?

For the first time Duckett doubted the sagacity of Jake Flanner. For the first time he began to think of that money he had put away. He had enough to live as he lived for a year, perhaps two . . . and two years was an almost immeasurable distance in the day-to-day living of Johannes Duckett.

"I'm going to ride," he told himself.

Once formulated, the idea established itself in its own groove and began to develop.

Jake Flanner would have been surprised to discover that to Johannes Duckett he, Jake Flanner, meant no more than a horse Duckett might have ridden for a time. He had been a convenience over the last few years, but no more than that.

Flanner believed Duckett to be loyal to the death. Duckett considered Flanner a source of income . . . and now that source of income was endangered.

And, of course, there was the western slope of the Rockies.

17

My mouth was dry and my head was hot—
the trip down the mountain had taken a lot out of me. I
crouched there among the rocks and brush and studied
the layout below. I still couldn't make it out.

That spot on the back step was blood, sure as shootin'.
Somebody had caught one there, and I was praying it
wasn't the old woman or Pennywell. Search as I might I
couldn't find anybody hid out, but they'd be hard to find
until they moved . . . if they were there.

I'd lost a lot of blood and from the way I felt I knew
I was worse off than I'd thought. A couple of times there
my eyes kind of glazed over until I couldn't see except
through a mist. Leaning over I rested my arm on a boulder and my head on my arm. My breathing was hoarse
and rasping and I was sick.

Nothing moved down below, and I must have passed
out there for a few minutes. When I came out of it I was
still there, my head resting on that rock, but I felt like I
was dying. That made me mad.

Die? With that old lady in trouble? With that girl I'd
brought to the house in danger because of me? With my
friend's ma down there, maybe about to get killed? And
yes, I'll sure be honest with myself—a whole lot of the
reason I was mad and surely determined to live was Jake
Flanner. I could hear his voice again, tellin' them to do
me in. All right, Jake, I said to myself. You want Logan
Sackett dead. You want him dead but you're going to
have to go all the way to make it happen.

So I forced my head up and slid down to a better way

144

of sittin'; through that brush, I watched the house. Below me I could see a sort of slide through the rocks. It was too steep to walk down, but a man lyin' flat on his back could maybe drop down fifteen or twenty feet lower, if he was careful.

Easing myself around, I got my legs stretched out. With a rifle in one hand and the crutch in the other I moved myself between two bushes and under the edge of a boulder and slid, using the crutch and rifle to keep me from going too fast. As it was I stopped with a hard jolt against a slab of rock and, worst of all, I'd made some dust.

Now I was closer down. I checked my guns to be sure I had them loaded, then I felt of my cartridge belt and didn't like what I found. I had eleven cartridges left for my pistol, and in my pockets I had a couple more rounds for the rifle. This here was not going to be any long fight.

Fogged though my thinkin' was, the more I studied that layout, the more sure I was that there was somebody inside who shouldn't be, that ma and them were dead or prisoners. Surely somebody would have come out that door otherwise.

Or else there was somebody on the hill behind me.

Now that was a thought. Maybe somebody back yonder had me right in their sights. Turning my head, I peered back up the mountain, but if they were right above me they couldn't see me at all. Suddenly I saw something I couldn't have seen from where I'd been until I slid.

There was a man's body—alive or dead there was no way of knowing—sprawled in front of the bunkhouse. I couldn't see it well but it surely looked like Al Fulbric. Regardless of who it was, there'd obviously been a fight. If that was Al, and I was sure it was, then somebody would have come for him.

The day had drawn on, and the sun was warm on my shoulders, but I wasn't feeling much but the warmth and the sickness that was in me. The house and the corrals down there seemed to waver, like there was heat waves

145

between us. From time to time I ran my hands over the rifle. It was reality, it was something tangible, something I knew. Squinting my eyes I peered down there. Somebody had to come down, somebody had to come out of the house. Then I'd know.

Suddenly my eyes caught movement, something out there on the road. Turning my head stiffly I peered, scowling, trying to see through the delirium that was in me.

It was a horse. It was a black appaloosa.

Only one man sat a horse like that, only one horse I'd ever seen looked like that. Far enough off so's I could just make him out, Milo Talon was riding up to a trap. Riding to his death from the guns that waited inside. Somehow he had to be warned, somehow he had to be told. I had no idea who was inside or how many there were, but I was sure there were too many. There'd been eight men including Flanner in the group that jumped me. Eight men in there with guns, just waiting for Milo or me.

If I fired a shot the chances were I'd never get off that slope alive. The only reason I'd made it so far was that they didn't know I was there, and if I moved they'd nail me instantly. But I knew I was surely going to do it because Milo was my friend and I wasn't about to see him shot down as he rode up, unsuspecting.

Unsuspecting? Well, maybe not. Milo never rode anywhere without being alert. He was like me, like a wild animal. He was always ready to cut and run or to fight.

He was only some three hundred yards off now, and you could bet they had him in their sights. My rifle tilted and I fired into the air. He slapped spurs to his horse, went down on the far side, and left there with bullets kicking all around him. And me, I went down off that mountain.

Nobody needed to tell me that I was walking into hell, nobody needed one word to tell me that ridge where I'd been holed up was going to be split wide open with rifle fire. If I died it was going to be gun in hand, boots on and walking, so I half ran, half slid off that hill, coming down like a madman.

I hit ground knees bent, heels dug in, with bullets kicking dust all around me. My mind was a blur but I went for that door and hit it with my shoulder. Like I said, I'm a big man and strong, and even weak as I was I tore that door loose and plunged into the kitchen. A sandy-haired man with a double-barrel shotgun was right square in front of me and I banged a shot at him, then lunged on in, jerking up the muzzle of my rifle. It missed his throat and tore his nose wide open and he screamed like a scared woman. I came around with the butt and there was a dull *thunk* as he hit the floor under my feet.

In the next room there was a sudden explosion, a yell, and I shifted the rifle to my left hand, grabbed up the shotgun, and plunged into the living room.

There were four men there and Em Talon and Pennywell lying in a corner. Pennywell seemed to have a bloody lip. I swung that shotgun around and let go with both triggers at twelve-foot range. She boomed like a cannon and the room was so full of smoke that my eyes stung with it. My head was buzzing and my knees felt like they were going to go any minute but I levered shot after shot into the smoke where those men were.

A man rushed through the smoke, six-gun in hand, his hat gone, hair wild, his blue eyes staring. I was to his right and he looked at me and swung the gun at me. I threw the shotgun at his face and followed it in. I had the rifle but I forgot it. I just taken a swing with my big right fist and clobbered him right over one of those blue eyes. His knees started to go and I taken that rifle in both hands and took a full swing at his belly with the butt. He folded like a wet sack and when he hit the floor on his knees I booted him in the face.

Staggering, I went down. My knees hit, and I lunged to get up and fell down. I tried to get up and rolled over in time to see a man come busting in from the front door.

He was a square-built man in a red-checkered shirt and he had a gun. He seen me and he throwed down on me. I figured he had me dead to rights. I looked square into that pistol and knew I'd bought it, but my whole life didn't pass in front of me. All I could think of was getting up and at him, knowing I'd never make it in time.

Behind me a gun boomed, then boomed again. That man stood up on his tiptoes, his gun dribbled from fingers gone rubber, and he fell all in one piece. As I turned my head, there was Em Talon holding a big Dragoon Colt she'd had hid somewhere in the folds of her dress.

Next thing I knew Pennywell was beside me, hauling me over to the wall, and the room was quiet. After a bit there was a moan . . . and it was me. Then somebody said, "Don't shoot! For God's sake, don't shoot!" And a man, bloody and dying, staggered past me to the door.

A window opened and the smoke started to suck out and the air cleared up. Three men were on the floor, but what shape they were in I don't know. They just laid there as Em knelt alongside of me and stared down at me. "You come just right, boy, you surely did. They got Barnabas tied up and they've shot Al."

"Milo's here. I shot to warn him."

"Milo? Then they better hunt cover."

They never tried to move me. They fetched a pillow for my head and they bathed my wounds that had tore loose and after a while they fed me some broth. Part of my weakness was just sheer hunger, but the blood I'd lost had done me no good.

Of the three men on the floor two of them were dead. One of them had caught most of the shotgun blast and the other had taken two forty-fours from Em's Dragoon Colt.

The man I'd hit in the belly with the rifle butt was still alive although he was in bad shape. The others, one way or another, got out of the house and we never did know what became of them. Anyway, they were gone and

148

there was no sign of Flanner. He'd been there, but crippled or not, he was gone before the shooting was over.

Em told me three of them had been down on their knees at loopholes letting Milo ride up. Somebody among them knew who he was and Flanner wanted him dead. With Em and Barnabas prisoners they expected to force one or the other to sign over the MT to them.

Three weeks I lay abed, waited on by Pennywell and Em. Three weeks when I lay mighty weak and came close to cashing in. Barnabas, Milo, and Al Fulbric rode into town but the Flanner outfit had scattered.

Albani Fulbric had been shot, all right, and had him a concussion, but no more than that and a minor flesh wound that gave him no trouble.

With Barnabas and Milo around things were back to normal. Al taken it easy a few days and then he set to and worked like the hand he was. I was the only one laid up, and I was sick enough so I scarcely knew where I was or what was keeping for the first ten days.

With the return of the Talon boys the house took on a new air. It surely didn't seem like that house was too big for them. They sang and roughhoused and told stories of the years between when they had been apart. Barnabas had traveled in Europe, had served in the army of France, and he was an educated man. Lyin' there in bed I listened to the easy flow of his talk and for the first time felt envy of another man.

When I was a boy yonder in the mountains we had to walk or ride miles to the nearest school, and often enough there was work to keep us from it, and nobody to make us go when there wasn't. We youngsters tried to duck out of school whenever possible, and it shamed me to think there were now youngsters who knew more than me, who could write better and read better.

I had never given thought to it before, and I could work as well as any man, but then I began to notice men like

149

me ending up setting by with nothing to live on while others had a-plenty. Barnabas had plenty of schooling, and even Milo had a good bit. I didn't know nothing but how to use a gun, ride a horse, and track game . . . or men.

Jake Flanner had disappeared. So had Johannes Duckett. Nobody had seen either one, and that tough lot who were hired by Flanner had all shaken the dust of the country from their hocks. The Flanner saloon and hotel had been taken over by Dorothy Arribas, while Con Wellington had opened his store full blast and was doing a good business.

But lyin' up like I was I done some thinking, and I wasn't at all sure those two were gone. A man as anxious to get even as Flanner, who'd done as much and spent as much, wasn't about to quit while losing. As for Duckett, he seemed ready to do whatever Flanner wanted.

Pennywell, she was around and about. She'd put up her hair and she was making eyes at all three of us, although the Talon boys the most. Em watched it and she was amused more than anything else. Barnabas didn't seem to be aware of her as more than just another person around, but Milo, I seen him looking her over once or twice.

Em had been to town, bought herself dress material, and was sewing up some new duds for herself. The boys shaped up the place and the cattle were loosed on the open range to get the best of the grass that was left.

I lay back in bed and stared up there at the ceiling wondering what was next for me. I never gave thought to it before, taking things as they came, but here I was laid up, mending slowly but surely, but seeing this big house around me and those folks. There was a strong feeling between Milo and Barnabas . . . brothers they were, and different as two men can be, and as boys they'd fought like cats and dogs, or so they said, but it was good

150

to see them now. They made a team, the two of them, and between them the old Empty began to shape up.

Maybe I lay abed a mite longer than needful. It was simply that I hated to leave that old house, Pennywell and Em and all of them. My own family busted up early, going off in different directions. We had a strong feeling for kinfolk in trouble, but my own family had scattered to the winds. Even Nolan, who was my twin brother, I'd not seen in a coon's age.

But the time had come for ridin' and one morning I rolled out of bed and put on my hat. Seems like in cow country a man always puts on his hat first. I slid into my jeans, and pretty raunchy they were, although Em and Pennywell had each taken a hand at putting them in shape. My shirt was patched up—Em had wanted to give me one of the boys' shirts but it wouldn't fit no way. I was too big in the shoulders and chest for either of them.

I was on my feet and slinging my gun belt around my hips when Pennywell came in. She taken one look and called out, "Em! Mrs. Talon! Logan is up!"

Em Talon came in and taken a long look at me. "Well, I knew I wasn't going to keep no Sackett in bed for long. Come on down, son, and have you some breakfast. You need to get some red meat into you, for blood. You lost a-plenty."

"Yes, ma'am," I said, and went.

18

For three days I did nothing but sit on the porch and look down the road toward Siwash. Everything was moving along on the Empty—the cattle were grazing on the prairie grass where they had not been able to graze freely since Flanner came into the country. The place was getting fixed up, and Em was for the first time looking kind of easy in the mind. She was sleeping all night, and so was Pennywell.

The Talon boys were out on the range most of the time, branding calves and picking up what mavericks they could find left over from the years since the Empty had been properly worked.

Me, I sat there on the porch and tried to think out what was in the thoughts of Jake Flanner and Johannes Duckett. Yet my mind kept straying down the trail to California. Soon I'd be well enough to go there. There was nothing to keep me longer. The boys were back, Em Talon was in good shape, and nobody would try to take the Empty with even Milo around. I'd seen Milo in action a time or two and knew he could handle whatever came his way.

In the three days of sitting on the porch I saw nothing to worry a man. In fact I saw nothing but grass and cows, with a few white clouds lazing it across a blue sky. On the fourth day I went out to the corral when the boys were topping off their horses. I was getting restless. Soon I'd be getting hog-fat with just setting by.

I taken up a rope, shook out a loop, and caught up that roan horse. He dodged around a bit but once the loop settled over his neck he stood by. I petted him a mite and talked to him, fed him a carrot, and slapped the saddle on him. He humped his back a mite, but by this time we'd become right friendly and he didn't feel like offering much of an argument. Anyway, I'd had it out with him before this and he knew who was boss.

Pennywell came to the door, drying her hands on a dish towel. "Logan Sackett, you must be a great big fool to try to ride in your condition. You tie that horse up and come in here!"

"Time for me to be headin' down the trail, ma'am. I never stay long in one place, and I've been around here a sight too long."

" 'Rolling stones gather no moss,' " she said pertly.

"I never saw moss grow on anything but dead wood and half-buried rocks," I said, "and anyway, a wandering bee gets the honey."

"A lot of honey you've had!"

"That's because you kept your eyes on Milo," I said, grinning at her. "An' I don't blame you. He's a sight prettier than me!"

"Depends on who's looking," she said. She watched me swing the horse around. "Where you all goin'? Em's in town. She's goin' to be mighty upset."

"Who rode with her?" Suddenly I was scared. "She wasn't alone, was she?"

"Who is there? Barnabas went to the mountains after a deer, an' Milo, him and Al, they went scouting the grass in the high meadows. Anyway, Em can take care of herself."

I taken up my saddlebags and slapped them over the saddle, then my rifle. "You tell the boys I said so long," I said. "I'll see Em in Siwash."

Swinging into the saddle I taken off down the trail to Siwash. Maybe it was because I'd been sick, but I was scared. Em had gone off alone, and that was what Flanner would be waitin' for. The boys figured he'd left the country, but not me. He was a vengeful man, and she'd crippled him bad. But he'd been whipped in what he'd tried against her. Maybe he had left the country but I didn't believe it.

The roan had been in the corral for a while and he was ready to go, so we taken the trail to Siwash and I scouted for sign of Em. Most of the time I'd been watching that trail, but a time or two I'd gone inside or out back and on one of those times she had taken out for town.

In no time at all I picked up mule tracks. She was walking him along, paying no mind to anything it seemed like. Anyway, from the steps of that mule she'd been letting him make his own speed, which was a bit slower than slow. That mule had no business anywhere and he was in no hurry to get there.

Meanwhile I swept the country toward Siwash, studying for sign. Nothing and nobody. Not even a dust cloud. Overhead the sky was still a clear blue dotted with fleecy clouds like lambs on a blue pasture. The roan taken me down into a hollow, then up the other side, and I'd gone several hundred yards when it came to me that the tracks were gone . . . played out.

I rode on a mite farther, still studying for sign, but there was nothing. That old woman and her mule were suddenly leaving no tracks at all. Town was only a half mile farther so I booted that roan and we went into town a-flyin'.

The first person I saw was Dolores Arribas. "You seen Em Talon?" I asked her.

"She ain't in town. If she was she'd have come to see me."

Con Wellington came to the door, his store apron on. "She hasn't been in," he said. "I've been expectin' her."

"You," I said to them, "you find her if she's in town, I mean you go to every door. You be mighty damn sure

154

she ain't here, because when I come back I'll be hunting mean."

Swinging the roan around I hightailed it back down the trail to where her trail wiped out. I found tracks before she reached the shallow bottom I'd crossed when her tracks disappeared, but I found none on the other side. She was gone.

She'd disappeared like she'd turned ghost or something. I could believe that of her, but not of her mule. A mule is a notional sort of crittur and that mule wasn't going to vanish . . . not before dinner time, anyway.

A quick swing up the draw, scouting for tracks, showed nothing at all. Not a turned grass blade, nothing. Then I went back to the trail and set my horse a-studying the premises. Folks just don't vanish; so somehow, some way, she'd been made to disappear . . . but how? This time when I gave study I wasn't looking for her tracks, I was looking for any kind of sign, anything at all.

I'd gone over that ground two or three times before I seen it, a straight line in the dust almost under the edge of some prickly pear and right in the bottom of the draw.

Now who would draw such a line? And for what? I studied it as I sat my saddle, and I came no nearer to guessing the cause of it. Getting down, I trailed the reins of the roan and studied the ground. There was an area about twelve by twenty that was totally free of tracks except for those made by my own horse as I rode to Si-wash.

Turning down the draw I stopped and studied the sand before I taken a single step. There was sand, a few scattered rocks, and some brush, nothing much to attract the attention. Yet some of the grass was kind of pushed down, and the leaves of some sunflowers were bruised and the flowers crushed. Something had pressed them down, something heavy, but what it was or how it had been done, I couldn't guess.

Wandering on down the draw about a hundred yards, I

found here and there some scratch marks in the sand like somebody had brushed out tracks. Now I'd done that a time or two myself but it never fools a good tracker because he will ask himself why the scratch marks or brush marks or whatever? You don't need hoof tracks or foot tracks to follow a trail. All a body needs are the indications that somebody passed that way, and most of the ways a man can brush out a trail show up just as well as his tracks.

The draw merged into a wider one that turned off to the southeast, and there around the corner I found where several horses had been tied . . . at least three, I guessed. There were several cigarette butts, like one of the men had been holding the horses or staying with them at least.

Up the draw I found what I was hunting—a mule track among the horse tracks as they went away. It taken no great figuring to see the mule was led. It might have been a pack mule except that Em Talon rode a mule and I knew the tracks her mule left.

Putting a toe to the track, I squinted at it, then sized up the other horse tracks one by one. Now a track of man or beast reads as plain as a signature to a good reader of sign. By the time I'd followed on a ways I knew each of those horses . . . and one of them was the horse ridden by Jake Flanner when he gave me the beating and left me for dead in the mountains.

Turning around I walked back to my roan, gathered the reins, and stepped into the saddle.

It was a long trail. They hadn't killed Em outright so it looked to be some plan of torture or ransom or something of the kind. Knowing what I did about Flanner I knew Em could not expect to get out of it alive . . . and I knew she knew it.

Fortunately, I was on the trail, and I was on it sooner than they figured anybody would be. I'd ridden the owlhoot trail too long not to know about every dodge a man can use, and it hadn't taken me long to work out their

156

direction. The way I surmised, they'd not expect pursuit before nightfall when Em didn't return to the Empty.

The sun was slanting down already, but it didn't look like I was more than a couple of hours behind them, and I could follow a trail like the one they now left with my horse at a gallop. The strides of their horses were longer. They were making good time now, but I could see the mule was making trouble. He was hanging back, and I hoped they wouldn't lose patience and shoot the old fellow. Em set store by that beast.

Now the route left the draw and taken off across the plains, cutting in closer and closer to the hills. It was an area I'd never seen and knew nothing about. I kept watch as far ahead as I could, knowing they might come in sight and they might also lay ambush for me. There was no dust clouds, nothing. Within an hour I'd gained on them. Some of the tracks were right fresh, but it was coming on for sundown and once it grew dark I'd lose the trail. And night would give Jake Flanner time to work on Em.

By this time the boys at the ranch would be getting restless with Em gone and me taking off like that. Pennywell would know I'd been scared for her, and the boys would come on into town to find out what had happened. Daybreak, at the latest, would see them fogging it down the trail after me—and the trail I left behind they could follow with ease.

One thing was sure. They were headed for someplace they knew. They were riding right into the hills now, not looking around for an opening, but riding toward some place they knew about. And I knew nothing about this country. The last tracks I could see were pointed into the hills, and sure enough, a canyon opened its jaws at me as I rode up. There didn't seem much chance they'd cut off to right or left, so I rode in and drew up, listening.

Now a canyon carries sound, and I did not want them to hear me. I sat very still, listening. Nothing . . . just nothing at all. A night bird cried somewhere, but that was

157

all. I searched the gray sky where a few stars appeared for the vague trail that smoke might make, and I studied the canyon walls for a reflected glow from a fire.

Nothing. . . .

It gave me an uneasy feeling. There was a coolness coming out of that canyon, and no smell of smoke. After a bit I walked my horse a dozen yards farther and stopped just short of where the canyon narrowed down. I stepped down from the saddle and with the most careful touch ever I touched the sand. Inch by inch I worked my way across the narrow opening. Forward, then back. There were no tracks in the sand.

Leading my horse I walked back to the mouth and went off to the right-hand shoulder of the canyon. There I peered up, looking for some opening in the dark wall of the trees that would show a trail. Sometimes there is a narrow gap against the sky . . . but this time there was nothing.

On the left it looked to be the same thing, and then I caught a faint odor of something that wasn't the damp coolness of green grass, brush, and trees.

Dust. . . .

I kneeled on the ground and felt with my fingers. Grass . . . wild flowers, and then a narrow trail, and in it my fingers felt out the vague pattern of hoofs.

For a moment there I stood with my hand on the pommel, my head leaning against the saddle. I was tired . . . almighty tired. This was the first time I'd been out since I'd been shot, and it was no time to be making a long, hard ride through mountains.

Pulling myself up into the saddle I let the roan have his head. "Let's see where they go," I said quietly. "Come on, boy, you've got to help me."

He taken off up the trail. I knew he could smell those other horses, and it is horse instinct to be with others of his kind, so I had a hunch I could trust that roan to take me to them once I had him on the right trail. He started along, walking fast. Loosening the grip of the scabbard on my Winchester, I taken the thong off my six-shooter. Somewhere up ahead those men had an old woman of my own family. All right . . . the kinship was distant, but it was there, and we'd talked together, drunk coffee together, fought enemies side by each.

We topped out on a rise and I made it quick over to the other side, not wanting to leave any target on the ridge. Ahead of me was a meadow, tall grass all silver in the rising moonlight. Silver but for one dark streak where riders had brushed off the dew of night. I trotted my horse, knowing in that damp grass it would make no sound to be heard farther than the creak of my saddle.

Ahead of me was a grove of aspen, big stuff, much larger than a man was usually likely to see. I rode to the edge of the grove and drew up to the white trunks ghostly in the beginning moonlight. We were high up, nothing but spruce and timberline above us.

Something was beginning to nag at my memory, and I couldn't place it. We'd come a good distance since I picked up the trail near Siwash . . . I'd make a guess at twenty miles. I was all in and the roan was beginning to lag, but there weren't too many groves of aspen that grew to this size. Aspen start to decay at the heart when they get too big, although I've seen some that didn't.

Looking up the mountain I could see timberline up there, not more than a thousand feet above me with a thick stand of spruce in between. There was a snaggly old tree up there that looked almighty familiar in a lopsided sort of way. And that was the trouble . . . everything looked kind of back-side to.

It came to me all of a sudden as I sat there on the roan just letting it soak in.

This was the old Fiddletown Mine country.

The Fiddletown had been a hideout for outlaws almost from discovery. There'd been several mines of the name, I guess, but this one was named by an Arkansas hillbilly who killed a man in a knife fight down near Cherry Creek. He took to the hills to hide out and discovered gold. There wasn't much gold but the country was mighty pretty, so Fiddletown Jack, as they called him, built himself a cabin and worked his mine, piling up a little gold against the time when it would be safe to come out. From time to time some friends of his holed up with him, and one of them, hunting Fiddletown's gold cache, was killed by Jack. But Jack was killed by the would-be thief's partner. After that, even outlaws shied away from the place for six or seven years, but from this moment to that somebody would hide out there for a while. I'd spent three weeks there one time . . . but that was years back. I hadn't heard tell of the place since then, and it was a way back yonder in the hills and an unlikely place to go.

I walked the roan on a couple of hundred yards and then drew up and got down. For a moment there my knees buckled and I feared I was about to fall, but I had me a grip on the old apple and I hung on until I got over the dizzy spell and the weakness.

I tied the roan there, leaving him room enough to nibble around on the brush, and then I shucked my Winchester and began to Injun through the aspens and spruce toward the cabins.

There was a bunkhouse yonder, the opening of the tunnel, a root cellar where Fiddletown had stored his moonshine, and there were a couple of old log cabins caved in by the heavy snows. It often got fourteen or fifteen feet deep through here, and deeper in the hollows. This was high country . . . more than ten thousand feet up.

First off I hunted their horses. I wanted an idea as to how many there were. I wanted that old lady out of there but getting myself killed wasn't going to help her none.

Three horses and a mule. I found them in a corral beyond the bunkhouse, but I stayed away, looking at them from a distance.

Three horses . . . was one a pack horse? Yet there had been at least three riders around the draw where they'd grabbed Em. Edging closer, and keeping shy of the corral where the horses might warn them, I worked up under the eaves of the bunkhouse. Making my way along the wall, close under the overhang of the low roof, I reached a window. It was so dirty and cobwebby I had trouble seeing through, but the first thing I saw was Em.

It gave me a lift just to see her. She was sitting up straight and tall. There was an ugly bruise on the side of her face where she must have been hit the time she was grabbed, hours ago, and there was a cut on her lip. She'd been hurt, but the fire was there, and the contempt she felt for them.

It was quiet inside and I could see none of the men I was hunting. I could make no move until I knew where every man-jack of them was. I didn't dare step into that cabin with Em in the line of fire or I'd just get her killed, and probably me, too. The worst of it was one of them might be outside somewhere on watch. If I started in he could take me from behind. My rifle shifted to my left hand while I checked to make sure my six-gun was there. It was.

Crouching down, I went under the window to look in from the other side. It was so dirty I could just barely make out one man sitting on the far side of the table from Em. He was talking to somebody else who was out of sight, so that accounted for two of them.

Em didn't seem in any immediate danger, but how could a body tell? I couldn't hear anything but a mumble of voices, but I couldn't feature them keeping her around long. Flanner wasn't fool enough to imagine he could scare the Talon boys into anything, and if he tried to get them to sign the ranch over to save their ma he'd still have them to deal with after.

Whatever he intended to do, he would do here.

I backed off from the cabin and got back to the stable.

Then I began an inch-by-inch check to see where the other man was. At least to find out if he was outside the house. None of them could be made out from that window.

Nobody was in the old stable, nor in the entrance to the mine tunnel. I worked my way around the place, moving, listening, then moving again.

There was only the one door and one window in the cabin. Squatting down among some rocks, I gave study to the situation. I had to get them out of there. There was no other way to do it—and when they came clear of the door I'd have to be shooting. It was no small thing to tackle three tough, well-armed men, and I was going to give them no more chance than they'd give me. I was sure that all three of them were in the crowd that beat me and left me for dead yonder over the mountains, so I'd get a little of my own back.

They had them a mite of fire going as the night was cold at that altitude. If I could get on the roof . . .

There was no chance of that. They'd hear me right off and shoot me to pieces before I could nail even one of them. They weren't pilgrims, who'd come running outside to see who or what was up there. They'd just go to shooting right through the roof . . . I'd done it myself, a time or two. A forty-five bullet will go through six inches of pine, and that roof was nothing but poles with a thin covering of grass and some dirt.

So I went back to the stable and got me a rope off one of the horse's rigs. I taken that rope, edged around in the darkness, measured the distance with my eyes, and built me a loop. Then I stepped back and roped that pipe they had for a chimney. I gave her a good yank and it came loose and there was a yell from inside. I stepped back into the deeper shadows, then ran around to the front door.

By the time I got there that cabin was filling up with smoke and those boys came out of there a-running. The first one was a man I'd seen before but never had his name. He was a big-chested man, showing a little belly over his gun belt. He came running outside, gun in hand, ready to drop whatever showed, but I wasted no time. Throwing up my Winchester, cocking as I lifted it, I shot him right in the belly. He heard the click of my hammer coming back and he let go with a shot that exploded before he wanted, my bullet knocking him back a step where the second one nailed him.

The light went out inside the cabin and then another man came out. I fired a quick shot at the vague outline of his figure and missed, and two bullets clipped brush near me. I ran at the cabin, thinkin' of Em. I heard a bullet thud into the logs just as I reached it, and I jumped inside. The cabin was filled with smoke, but I saw Em struggling against the ropes. I couldn't really see her but I made out a dim outline that had to be her.

My knife was razor sharp and I cut her loose. "Watch it!" she whispered hoarsely. "Flanner, Duckett, an' Slim are outside."

I'd figured on three . . . and that made four. There might be another around.

"Em," I whispered, "can you crawl?"

She went to the floor near me and started for the door. They'd be laying for us outside, so I taken up a chair and heaved it out the door, then plunged out and began raking the area with rifle fire to cover Em's escape.

There were a couple of shots and then a whole lot of silence and I saw Em making for the corral. Nobody fired, so I backed up, trying to see all ways at once. The moon was getting up over the shoulder of the mountain now, so we got back against the corral's indefinite shadow and crouched there.

"You take care of yourself, Logan," Em said. "I got the dif'rence now," and she showed me the big old Dragoon Colt that she must have caught up before leaving the cabin.

The moon was shining over half the clearing now and we could see the body of the man I'd shot lying out there in the open. He wasn't dead but he was going to wish he was. I'd seen men shot in the gut before and took no pleasure in it. Nothing else moved. I studied the cast of the moonlight and decided we were all right as long as we stayed still. Leaning my Winchester against the poles of the corral, I shucked my six-shooter and waited for something to move out there.

It was almighty still. I could hear the chuckle of the water in the creek some distance off, and once in a while a horse shifted his feet in the corral. I guessed that the fire had gone out or died down because smoke no longer came from the cabin that did duty as a bunkhouse. The door gaped open, a black rectangle that suggested a place a body could hide and stand off a crowd, but I liked the open where a body could move.

You know something? It was beautiful. So still you could hear one aspen leaf caressing another, the moon wide and white shining through the leaves, and just above the dark, somber spruce, bunched closely together, tall and still like a crowd of black-robed monks standing in prayer.

And the old buildings, the fallen-in cabins, the log bunkhouse, the black hole of the mine tunnel. A bird made a noise, inquiring of the night. There was nothing else but an occasional rustling from the aspen whispering together like a bunch of schoolgirls. And me there with a gun in my hand, and Em by my side.

A voice spoke, a low voice, not over ten yards off. It was a voice I'd heard only once that I could recall, but I knew it for Johannes Duckett.

"Logan Sackett?"

I wasn't about to answer, nor to shoot until I heard him out. I had his position spotted the instant he spoke, but I learned long since not to shoot too soon or without reason. So I waited.

"This is Johannes Duckett. I am pulling out. I have had enough of this. I never wanted to shoot at Emily Talon, and I will not. This is Jake Flanner's fight."

There was a pause, during which I waited, listening to see if it was a cover for movement. Then he said, "I want to move now, and I don't want to get shot when I do."

I said nothing, but then he commenced to move, and I could hear him drawing back. The sounds slowly drifted away farther off down the hill, and then there was silence.

Two men left. . . . I got up slowly, standing by the corner post of the corral, which was taller than me.

Suddenly a match flared in the cabin, a lamp was lit. I heard the tiny click of the chimney as it was fitted to the lamp again. A man moved within the cabin and we heard the thump of a crutch, but then a chair was drawn back and we heard the creak as a heavy man sat down.

"Em," I whispered, "he's gotten into the cabin."

"You don't do nothin' foolish, boy."

"There's another one, Em. I think he's out around here somewhere."

"You do what you have to, son. I'll watch that other one."

"Jake Flanner is a talker, Em. I think he wants to talk to me. I don't believe he'll try killing me until he's had his say."

"All right."

I turned and walked across the open ground toward the bunkhouse. My six-shooter was in my hand, but as I stepped inside I dropped it into the holster. I had listened for sound outside, but heard nothing.

Jake Flanner had gotten to his feet and was leaning on his crutches, favoring one side as he always seemed to do. There was a pistol showing in its holster, and I knew he carried another one inside his coat. He moved his arm, letting me glimpse the butt of that hideout gun.

Why?

Every sense alert, I waited. He was the talker, not me. I was tired, dead tired. As I stood there, feet apart, hands hanging, I felt all sickish and weak. If I didn't get better soon I'd never get to California.

Suddenly Jake's voice rang out of the stillness. "You've given me a lot of trouble, Sackett. I wish you had come to work for me that first day."

"I never work for no man. Not with a gun."

"But why against me? I did nothing to you."

"I didn't like the way your boys set after that girl."

"Her? Really? But she's nobody, Sackett. She's just a broken-down nester's daughter."

"Everybody is somebody to me. Maybe she don't cut no ice where you figure, Flanner, but she's got the right to choose her man when she's ready, not to be taken like that."

He laughed, his eyes glinting. "I heard you were a hard man, Sackett, and so you've proved to be. I would never have suspected you of chivalry."

"I don't know what that means, Flanner. I only know she was a poor kid, all wet from the rain and scared from runnin', and that Spivey—"

"But that's over, Sackett. Spivey is dead. Why did you take up for Em Talon?"

"Emily Talon is a Sackett. I don't need no more reason than that."

He shifted his weight, leaning kind of heavy to one side, and that nagged at me. I don't know why except that I'm a suspicious man.

"Too bad, Sackett. We'd have made a team. You, Duckett, and me."

"Duckett is gone."

He was shocked. He stared at me. "What do you mean? You've killed him? But I heard no shot!"

"He just pulled out. He had enough, Flanner. He said he never did believe in going after Em Talon. He's gone. You're alone, Flanner."

He smiled then. "Oh? Well, if that's the way the cards fall." He moved up a little and turned a shade to one side. "Mind if I sit down, Sackett? These crutches—"

Jake Flanner hitched himself forward a little. Suddenly one of the crutches swung up and I shot him.

It was as fast and clean a draw as I ever made, but as that crutch swung up as though he were going to lay it on the table, I shot him right in the belly. My second shot hit the hand and wrist that held the crutch and he fell back against the chair, caught at it, and they fell together.

"You'd shoot a crip—?" His voice faded, but not the glow in his eyes. His crutches had fallen but his right hand was going toward the hideout gun.

There was a sudden *boom* from outside that could only be the Dragoon. "Everything's all right out here, Logan," Em said. "I taken this one out."

I just stood there gun in hand, watching him take hold of the butt of his hideout gun.

"Jake," I said, "I always wondered why you favored that one crutch over the other, and all of a sudden it come to me."

With my free hand I reached over and picked up the crutch. There was a rifle barrel right down the length of that crutch, and a grip trigger on the handle. All he had to do was swing that crutch up and squeeze her off. I'd heard of trick guns, belt-buckle guns and the like, but this one surely beat all.

His hand was drawing his hideout.

"You want another one, Jake? You're dead already, why make it worse?"

He looked at me. "Damn you, Sackett. An' damn that old lady, damn her to hell, she—"

"You were out of your class, Jake. No tin-horn's ever going to come it over a woman like that. She's the solid stuff, Jake, all the way through, and you were never anything but a cheatin' tin-horn four-flusher."

Em came in and stood by my side.

"I'm sorry for them knees, Jake Flanner," she said, "but you killed my man. You killed Talon, a better man than you could ever be."

"Damn you," he whispered, "I—"

He faded out and lay there, dead as a man could ever get, and the thing that hit me so hard was how such a man could cause the death of so much a better man like Talon.

"Em," I said, "there's nothin' more for us here. The boys will be worried. Let's mount up and ride back to the Empty."

"You look kinda peaked, son. Are you up to it?"

"If you can do it, I can do it, Em. Let's make some dust."

So we rode down the trail together, Em and me, and we met the boys a-comin' up.

ABOUT LOUIS L'AMOUR

"I think of myself in the oral tradition—as a troubadour, a village taleteller, the man in the shadows of the campfire. That's the way I'd like to be remembered—as a storyteller. A good storyteller."

It is doubtful that any author could be as at home in the world recreated in his novels as Louis Dearborn L'Amour. Not only could he physically fill the boots of the rugged characters he writes about, but he has literally "walked the land my characters walk." His personal experiences as well as his lifelong devotion to historical research have combined to give Mr. L'Amour the unique knowledge and understanding of people, events, and the challenge of the American frontier that have become the hallmarks of his popularity.

Of French-Irish descent, Mr. L'Amour can trace his own family in North America back to the early 1600s and follow their steady progression westward, "always on the frontier." As a boy growing up in Jamestown, North Dakota, he absorbed all he could about his family's frontier heritage, including the story of his great-grandfather who was scalped by Sioux warriors.

Spurred by an eager curiosity and desire to broaden his horizons, Mr. L'Amour left home at the age of fifteen and enjoyed a wide variety of jobs including seaman, lumberjack, elephant handler, skinner of dead cattle, assessment miner, and officer on tank destroyers during World War II. During his "yondering" days he also circled the world on a freighter, sailed a dhow on the Red Sea, was shipwrecked in the West Indies and stranded in the Mojave Desert. He has won fifty-one of fifty-nine fights as a professional boxer and worked as a journalist and lecturer. A voracious reader and collector of rare books, Mr. L'Amour's personal library of some 10,000 volumes covers a broad range of scholarly disciplines including many personal papers, maps, and diaries of the pioneers.

Mr. L'Amour "wanted to write almost from the time I could walk." After developing a widespread following for his many adventure stories written for the fiction magazines, Mr. L'Amour published his first full-length novel, *Hondo*, in 1953. Mr. L'Amour is now one of the four bestselling living novelists in the world. Every one of his more than 95 books are still in print and every one has sold more than one million copies. He has more million-copy bestsellers than any other living author. His books have been translated into more than a dozen languages, and more than thirty of his novels and stories have been made into feature films and television movies.

His hardcover bestsellers include *The Lonesome Gods; The Walking Drum,* his twelfth-century historical novel; *Jubal Sackett;* and *Last of the Breed.*

The recipient of many great honors and awards, in 1983 Mr. L'Amour became the first novelist ever to be awarded a Special National Gold Medal by the United States Congress in honor of his life's work. In 1984 he was also awarded the Medal of Freedom by President Ronald Reagan.

Mr. L'Amour lives in Los Angeles with his wife, Kathy, and their two children, Beau and Angelique.